3C

David Adjmi

A Samuel French Acting Edition

SAMUELFRENCH.COM
SAMUELFRENCH-LONDON.CO.UK

ISBN 978-0-573-70455-0

www.SamuelFrench.com
www.SamuelFrench-London.co.uk

For Production Enquiries

United States and Canada
Info@SamuelFrench.com
1-866-598-8449

United Kingdom and Europe
Plays@SamuelFrench-London.co.uk
020-7255-4302

Each title is subject to availability from Samuel French, depending upon country of performance. Please be aware that *3C* may not be licensed by Samuel French in your territory. Professional and amateur producers should contact the nearest Samuel French office or licensing partner to verify availability.

MUSIC USE NOTE

IMPORTANT BILLING AND CREDIT REQUIREMENTS

3C was first produced by Snug Harbor Productions/Steven Chaikelson and Kendra Bator, and presented by Piece by Piece Productions, Rising Phoenix Repertory (Daniel Talbott, artisitic director) and the Rattlestick Playwrights Theater (David Van Asselt, artistic director; Brian Long, managing director) at the Rattlestick Playwrights Theater in New York City on June 24, 2012. The performance was directed by Jackson Gay, with sets by John McDermott, costumes by Dana Botez, lights by Tyler Micoleau, sound by Matt Tierney, choreography by Deney Terrio, and hair and makeup design. The Production Manager was Tom Taylor and the General Manager was Eugenia Furneaux. The cast was as follows:

BRAD.......................................Jake Silbermann
LINDA.......................................Hannah Cabell
CONNIE.......................................Anna Chlumsky
MR. WICKER.......................................Bill Buell
MRS. WICKER.......................................Kate Buddeke
TERRY.......................................Eddie Cahill

CHARACTERS

BRAD – (M, late 20s/early 30s)

LINDA – (F, late 20s/early 30s)

CONNIE – (F, late 20's/early 30s)

MR. WICKER – (M, late 50s/late 60s)

MRS. WICKER – (F, late 50s/late 60s)

TERRY – (M, late 20s/late 30s)

SETTING

An apartment complex in Santa Monica, California.

TIME

1978

AUTHOR'S NOTES

I write for the musicality of the line, not grammatical correctness.

The rhythms of the play are not naturalistic. Please don't naturalize them. The play has a honed instability, like Romantic music, a kind of rubato.

A double slash (//) indicates either an overlap or a jump – i.e., no break between the end of one character's speech and the beginning of the following speech.

Speech in parentheses indicates either a sidetracked thought or footnote within a conversation, or a shift in emphasis with NO transition.

A STOP is a pause followed by either a marked shift in tone or tempo (like a cinematic jumpcut or a quantum leap) or no change in tempo whatsoever – somewhat like putting a movie on pause and then pressing play. These moments in the play are less psychological than energetic. They have a kind of focused yet unpredictable stillness, something akin to Martial Arts, where there is preparedness in the silence. Where a lunge or a swift kick can be delivered from seemingly out of nowhere – quickly, invisibly.

Sometimes sentences will abut with no period or punctuation This means you just keep talking without taking a beat for a period a comma.

SOME THOUGHTS ON *3C*

TONE

The tone of *3C* is a little tricky. Though it explores and samples tropes from sitcoms and farce (and can be at points pretty funny) the play is not exactly a comedy. And it's not really a drama, though it is in many ways an exploration of human anguish. The play – like the characters – is so flipped out by the human condition that it doesn't quite know how to feel about itself. It has a short-circuited, convulsive, somewhat manic-depressive quality. To this end there are mercurial shifts in tone that happen scene by scene, within scenes and between beats. The shifts are often abrupt and happen with no transition.

I've tried to delineate in the text as best as I could. Please use the text as a guide. It isn't a terribly good idea to cross out stage directions in this play – they offer a useful roadmap to its often very twisty terrain.

SPEED

3C is so much about panic and existential terror in the face of a profoundly toxic world. On the surface it seems kind of flat and lowbrow; but it's a reverse *trompe l'oeil* – the flatness is illusion. And for the play to work in production this tension between the surface banality and this underlying anxiety/horror must be present.

To this end, it is important to follow the rhythms of the play that way I've scored it out in the text. The anxiety gets shunted into a sort of a wild hydroplaning speed in the dialogue that is punctuated with abrupt shifts, and increasingly frightening gaps and silences. Please do attend to the very specific scoring in the text and do not cross out the stage directions.

A double slash (//) indicates either an overlap or a jump – i.e., no break between the end of one character's speech and the beginning of the following speech. I recommend learning the lines and the interruptions indicated by slashes at the same time. Please be very specific with the slashes. They inform the play's meaning and very specific sensibility.

Speech in parentheses indicates either a sidetracked thought within a conversation, or a shift in tone or emphasis.

Please do not add pauses or silences or beats where they aren't indicated in the script. The style of the play isn't naturalistic and there shouldn't be a lot of air inside sentences unless the script indicates it.

THREE'S COMPANY

Though the play is largely premised on the 1970s series *Three's Company*, please don't comment on the sitcom aspects of the play, or telegraph them in a goofy, broad way. The play borrows tropes from that series to subvert them, but it has its own life and its own idiom.

Don't feel compelled to recreate or pastiche the performances from *Three's Company*: Connie need not be 'jiggly'; Linda need not be 'sensible', etc. The characters in *3C* are drawy very differently; they are specific to this play and this particular world.

CONFUSIONS

No matter how ridiculous or absurd some of the "confusions" are they've got to be played completely straight – like Chekhov or Bergman – there needs to be that level of anguish, that sort of gravity. It should feel disorienting.

THE 'SCENE'

Mr. Wicker's scene with Linda near the end of Act One is – and is meant to be – jarring and disturbing. But it need not be sensationalized or played up for shock value in the staging. For the Rattlestick production it happened upstage, semi-concealed and it was still terribly (but for the play, appropriately) cringeworthy and awful. Use your judgment.

THANK YOUS (IN NO ORDER)

MCC Playwrights Coalition, Stephen Willems, New Dramatists, Polly Carl, Clubbed Thumb, Maria Striar, Playwrights Horizons, Jackson Gay, Judith Ivey, Josh Hamilton, Marin Ireland, Deney Terrio, Anna Chlumsky, Eddie Cahill, Laura Heisler, Hannah Cabell, Colleen Werthmann, Kate Buddeke, Jake Silbermann, Greg Keller, Laura Esterman, Marylouise Burke, Keith Reddin, Lisa Joyce, Bill Buell, Gary Wilmes, Darren Goldstein, Paul Rusconi, Heidi Schreck, and my ur-assistant Philip Gates. Special thank you to Kip Fagan for his incisive, dedicated work on this play over the course of several workshops. And to Adam Greenfield for rescuing an abandoned draft from my desk drawer. And to all the actors who participated in countless readings, workshops, etc. of this play who aren't mentioned here.

1.

(It's late morning. The place is a mess, half empty wine glasses, cigarette butts, vestiges of a party from the previous night. A "Bon Voyage Beverly" banner hangs above the door. **CONNIE** *is wearing a teddy, reads "Cosmo."* **LINDA** *is wearing a long T-shirt, a sports-type thing.* **LINDA** *is siphoning un-drunk wine from various glasses back into a half empty bottle.)*

LINDA. I'm so hung over.

CONNIE. *(encouraging)* You look splotchy.

LINDA. *(slightly stung)* So do you.

(**LINDA** *doesn't look over at her;* **CONNIE***'s offended.)*

CONNIE. You're not even looking.

LINDA. What are you reading?

CONNIE. *(reads, traumatized)* This lady was disfigured cause she burnt her bra. The whole house burned down, now the insurance people are after her. *(flips a page, anxious)* People lead such interesting lives. *(turns to* **LINDA**, *re: the funnel)* What's that //

LINDA. It's called saving money.

CONNIE. *(yikes)* You're so innovative.

(**CONNIE** *goes back to reading.)*

LINDA. Necessity is the mother of invention //

CONNIE. *(confused, oddly hurt)* I thought that was god the father. *(shrugs it off)* But I'm *fallen* What do I know. My dad used to say that to me all the time He was a minister //

LINDA. I didn't know that.

CONNIE. We're all fallen //

LINDA. I mean about your dad being a minister! //

CONNIE. He was good at sermons. *(uncanny moment)* You remind me of him. *(casual)* We need a vacation; I heard about this place on the news Love Canal It sounds romantic; maybe you can find a boyfriend.

LINDA. We can't afford a vacation; we can barely make rent.

CONNIE. *(hopeful)* Now that Beverly's gone maybe we can spend more time together. I've always wanted us to be close.

LINDA. *(warming up to it)* That sounds good.

CONNIE. *(losing focus)* It sounds ok.

LINDA. What should we do?

CONNIE. *(hopeful)* Maybe we can go double dating.

LINDA. I need to lose weight first.

CONNIE. You always say that.

LINDA. I can't date anyone looking like this.

CONNIE. You look great. You just need to get out and mingle.

LINDA. I know. I'm not as social as you are. *(beat)* How do you meet all these guys?

CONNIE. Well I used to go to this drug store and wait around in the parking lot; *(disappointed)* then they put up a no loitering sign.

(**CONNIE** *contemplates this, nonplussed.)*

LINDA. *(reacts)* Don't you think it's dangerous to date strange men?

CONNIE. *(matter-of-fact)* If you flirt you flirt with danger, I learned that the hard way.

LINDA. *(mild rebuke)* Connie, you have to be responsible //

CONNIE. My gramma used to say that.

LINDA. Hey did you pay the electricity bill?

CONNIE. I had to buy that coat.

LINDA. What *coat?*

CONNIE. With the zippers? that coat that was on sale?

LINDA. Connie, you don't even have a *job.*

CONNIE. *(hurt)* I had to quit, my boss was hitting on me!

LINDA. Well I just spent all that money on Beverly //

CONNIE. *(concerned)* I'll // chip in

LINDA. And we're two weeks behind on // rent!

CONNIE. *(mollifying)* We're not as behind as some people – 3F is behind two months and 6G I don't even know how long.

LINDA. (Who's in 6G //

CONNIE. That guy with the girlfriend But I think she left him //

LINDA. How do you know? //

CONNIE. Because he was having sex with me but she walked in) *Hey* you wanna go to the beach today?

*(**LINDA** gives her a look.)*

LINDA. I hate this apartment.

*(**LINDA** does an impromptu flower arrangement, **CONNIE** watches, quietly fascinated.)*

CONNIE. The flowers are all dying.

LINDA. I'll get new ones from the shop.

CONNIE. My grandma used to press flowers and put them in a book.

LINDA. We're getting zebra orchids in later today.

CONNIE. *(absorbed)* What are these?

LINDA. Delphiniums. They were gonna die so I brought them home.

CONNIE. Aren't they already dead once you cut them?

LINDA. Flowers don't die like that, they die more slowly.

CONNIE. *(concerned)* Like slow torture? Like China?

LINDA. The line between life and death isn't so clearcut for a flower //

CONNIE. Like *India*?

LINDA. *I don't know about India*!!

(**CONNIE** *watches her arrange the flowers.*)

CONNIE. *(contemplative)* Can they feel pain?

LINDA. What?

CONNIE. When you cut a flower does it hurt?

LINDA. They don't have developed nerve centers.

CONNIE. So?

LINDA. They're just stalks with petals //

CONNIE. *(horrified)* "Stalks with // *petals*"?

LINDA. Connie they don't have advanced cortical functions, they just do photosynthesis //

CONNIE. *(hurt)* Maybe flowers don't have a means to communicate pain – that doesn't mean they don't feel things. They're living beings, all living creatures feel things //

LINDA. I //

CONNIE. *(increasing hurt and indignation)* It's like what happened to Helen Keller //

LINDA. I don't // want to

CONNIE. I was in *Miracle Worker* in eighth grade. The whole society thought // she was –

LINDA. Helen Keller had a developed nervous system! //

CONNIE. So? //

LINDA. Flowers don't, they can live when you cut them, they // can

CONNIE. *(sarcasm)* Well you're just // soooo

LINDA. I just sat on gum //

CONNIE. EW! //

LINDA. *(holds up a condom)* (Oh no it's a used condom) //

CONNIE. *(private recollection)* (Aww) //

LINDA. *We have got to clean // this shit up!*

CONNIE. *(mimicking broadly) bleh bleh // bleh*

LINDA. *(pulls down the banner)* And when are we going to get a new roommate? Did you at least put an ad in the chronicle like I told you?

CONNIE. No one wants to live in Santa Monica, it's too far from West Hollywood.

LINDA. *(throws banner in the trash)* What's in West Hollywood?

CONNIE. *(matter of fact)* Shops.

LINDA. *(opening up)* I like shops.

CONNIE. *(brightening) Do you want to see my new coat?*

LINDA. I'm still mad at you How are we gonna make rent? //

CONNIE. (Here you want a triscuit?)

LINDA. I don't like the way I look today.

CONNIE. You're not fat //

LINDA. I *didn't say fat* //

CONNIE. *(appeasing)* That's what you always say I'm fat I don't like the way I look today //

LINDA. I'm gonna cut my hair //

CONNIE. Yeah you // should

LINDA. *What's wrong with my hair?* //

CONNIE. *(180 switch)* Nothing I love your hair!

LINDA. Should I cut it, do you think I should grow it out? //

CONNIE. No, yes –

LINDA. I think it looks good with my belt.

CONNIE. *(a terrified beat)* What //

LINDA. *My hair!*

CONNIE. *I miss Beverly!*

(STOP)

LINDA. There's gum embedded in the carpet.

CONNIE. Use goo gone.

LINDA. I'm not cleaning it.

CONNIE. We'll do it // together.

LINDA. I'm not cleaning it, I had to set the whole thing up practically by myself.

CONNIE. No one asked you to do that.

LINDA. I did it without having to be asked because I'm actually a responsible person.

(beat)

CONNIE. Maybe you need to experience more *things.* You need to experience life – *You should go dancing, you love to dance.*

LINDA. Will you stop putting your things on me!?

CONNIE. *(taking this literally)* I'm not putting my things on you //

LINDA. *And I'm not going out with anyone until I lose twenty pounds*!! *LEAVE ME ALONE.*

(pause)

CONNIE. *(tentative)* Are you sure you don't wanna see my new coat?

LINDA. *(holds her head)* I feel like shit.

CONNIE. Your face is all blue. *(sad)* I hope you don't have alcohol poisoning. They might have to give you a transfusion. I used to do that for my grandmother.

*(**LINDA** looks over at **CONNIE**; she doesn't know how to take this.)*

LINDA. You gave your grandmother a *transfusion?*

CONNIE. I gave her shots and things, she had diabetes. But then my mother refused to take care of her and we put her in a home. She died a few months later. I *never* forgave my mother. *(pause)* Well I forgave her but only years later, but we *never* spoke again.

*(**CONNIE** is lugubrious.)*

LINDA. I'm sorry //

CONNIE. Well I mean we speak but only on special occasions, you know, like on holidays and birthdays, but *that's it.*

LINDA. Oh.

(beat)

CONNIE. *(turns a page in her magazine)* Also we get our nails done every week //

LINDA. *(holding up her hand)* Do you like this shade It's iridescent.

(**CONNIE** *looks at her nails.)*

CONNIE. That's not for me.

LINDA. *(hurt)* The manicurist said it's the new style.

CONNIE. *(oddly disgusted)* I have learned to smell a rat when it comes to manicurists. *(***LINDA** *reacts, frightened)* But maybe Todd Stengler will like it.

LINDA. *(this upsets her)* I don't care if he does or if he doesn't.

CONNIE. Maybe he'll get turned on by it.

LINDA. Why do you keep mentioning Todd Stengler?

CONNIE. Because he has red pubes.

LINDA. I think you want him for yourself!

CONNIE. I think it's the other way around!

LINDA. I don't like *Todd*!

CONNIE. You always mention him.

LINDA. And what If I do? I have no chance with you around.

CONNIE. You do too.

LINDA. I'm ugly and I look like a dyke!

CONNIE. You are *not* a dyke.

(pause)

LINDA. I know what people say about me //

CONNIE. *What?* People // don't –

LINDA. *(hurt)* I know what people say.

(long pause)

CONNIE. You remind me of this friend I had, Tammy. She was traumatized. Then she realized she had to heal.

LINDA. How did she do it?

(**CONNIE** *stares blankly for a beat.)*

CONNIE. All I know is the anecdote.

(**CONNIE** *shrugs.)*

LINDA. I'm in a bad mood.

CONNIE. *(strained)* You're in a great mood.

LINDA. I get this way when I drink //

CONNIE. You can always cut // down

LINDA. I hope I don't have blood poisoning //

CONNIE. Do you want me to check your blood? I used to do that for my grandmother –

LINDA. My grandmother was sick too She had leukemia //

CONNIE. *(sadly)* My cat had leukemia //

LINDA. *My cat had cancer* //

CONNIE. *(excited by the coincidence)* My friend Nancy had // cancer!

LINDA. My cat's name was // Nancy!

CONNIE. *(nonsequitur)* Anyways I used to give her insulin shots //

LINDA. Your cat? //

CONNIE. No my grandma. She'd writhe around. She'd get really mad at me when I punctured the vein. I would say GRANDMA IT'S TIME FOR YOUR SHOT the way I saw Jack Lemmon do it on Quincy //

LINDA. Klugman //

*(**LINDA** grabs a bottle of liquor.)*

CONNIE. And then she died Did yours die?

LINDA. Mine lives in Larchmont //

CONNIE. (Larchmont is that like a time share?) //

LINDA. I need a scotch //

*(Doorbell rings. **LINDA** pours herself a drink. **CONNIE** sighs, answers door. **MR WICKER** enters.)*

CONNIE. *(glum)* Hey Mr Wicker.

WICKER. You girls are gonna pay the rent or what, it's the fourteenth //

CONNIE. We paid some of it.

WICKER. You've been late for the past three months.

LINDA. *(swilling liquor)* What about our faucet, do tenants not have rights?!

WICKER. I fixed that //

CONNIE. *(has a meltdown) It's still leaking!*

LINDA. We'll get the rent //

WICKER. I want it by the end of the // week!

*(**CONNIE** slams the door on **WICKER, LINDA** forages for more alcohol.)*

CONNIE. Well I don't know what the fuck we're // gonna do

LINDA. (Where's the Noilly // Pratt)

CONNIE. *(resentment)* I mean maybe I should have stayed at my job with my boss // groping at me

LINDA. *(swigs from the bottle)* And I'm sure you'll leave soon Just like Beverly left //

CONNIE. That's not // true!

LINDA. You have like a hundred boyfriends.

CONNIE. So? //

LINDA. So you'll marry one and I'll be left to rot and feed on my // own putrefaction!!

CONNIE. (I hurt my back playing limbo last night) //

LINDA. You'll get married and leave and I'll have to put another fuckin ad in the newspaper!

CONNIE. *(excited)* We could live here with you!

LINDA. *(confused) Who?*

CONNIE. *(annoyed)* Me and my *husband*!

LINDA. I don't want to live with you and your // husband.

CONNIE. *(clapping)* You could babysit! //

LINDA. *(offended)* I'm not gonna *babysit* //

CONNIE. *(hurt and angry) What, you wanna free ride? That's bullshit!*

LINDA. I want to live *alone!*

CONNIE. *(sweetly)* If flowers can be uprooted and live, so can *you*: live with *us* //

LINDA. I'm not a flower, I'm like Jo from little women // I'm independent

*(**BRAD** enters from the kitchen, naked but for a sock on his left foot.)*

CONNIE. *(delighted)* You're like Maria von Trapp: she made // playclothes out of

BRAD. Ow my *head* –

*(The girls scream "oh my god" "help"etc etc – terrified – which terrifies **BRAD**, who screams and runs back into the kitchen, banging his head on the door on his way back in.)*

(STOP)

LINDA. *(frightened) Who* are you?!

CONNIE. *(confused)* What are you doing in our kitchen?

BRAD. *(os; hungover)* I was at the party last night.

CONNIE. *(testing him) What party?*

BRAD. *(os)* I must've blacked out.

LINDA. Where are your clothes?

BRAD. *(os)* Um. I don't know exactly.

LINDA. Hold on.

*(**LINDA** hurriedly produces a towel, squeezes her eyes shut, hands it to him around the kitchen door.)*

BRAD. *(os)* I hope Terry's playing a joke on me //

LINDA. Terry in 4C We know Terry! //

CONNIE. Did we play limbo last night Was that you I was so wasted //

*(**BRAD** enters wearing the towel.)*

BRAD. Can I use your phone?

LINDA. Sure //

(He picks up the phone, dials.)

CONNIE. *(sings)* "LIMBO LIMBO" //

LINDA. *(random socializing)* Do you know Denny Tucker Were you at that party? //

CONNIE. Gosh Linda –

LINDA. I can't believe there was a naked man in our kitchen this whole time!

(Beat, **CONNIE** *contemplates the situation.)*

CONNIE. America has a lot of opportunities if you know where to look.

BRAD. Thanks for letting me use your phone.

*(***CONNIE** *smiles at* **BRAD***.)*

CONNIE. *(judgmental)* I don't know if I like his manners.

LINDA. He looks nice.

CONNIE. Appearances can be deceiving. On the other hand you can't judge a book by its cover.

LINDA. Connie that's the same thing.

BRAD. *(hangs up)* No answer.

CONNIE. He's not home? Maybe he's just passed // out

LINDA. He's probably just playing a joke on you //

CONNIE. Terry's a total joker.

BRAD. I just hope I wasn't mugged //

CONNIE. *(an aside)* I was mugged once and I'm still traumatized //

LINDA. Hey we don't even know your name //

BRAD. I'm Brad //

LINDA. I'm Linda and this is Connie.

CONNIE. *(correcting her) Con-nie.*

LINDA. That's what I said.

(beat)

CONNIE. You said *Com-mie.*

(A beat as **CONNIE** *rolls her eyes.* **LINDA** *looks confused.)*

BRAD. Thanks for the towel.

LINDA. So how do you know Terry?

BRAD. I met him when I got to town, I was down at the Rolley Pony // and

CONNIE. We call it The Pony.

BRAD. Well I was playing pool // and

CONNIE. We call it billiards //

BRAD. Huh? //

CONNIE. I'm just kidding. Look at your skin It's like the color of the sofa – I love when I match the furniture it gives me a sense of belonging.

BRAD. You two have a lot of energy.

LINDA. We get excited having company over.

CONNIE. Unless they're rapists.

LINDA. Do you have a girlfriend? //

CONNIE. You smell like jojoba.

BRAD. I don't know what // that is.

LINDA. What's your sign, I'm a Cancer //

BRAD. I //

CONNIE. Hey, let's put on music!

LINDA. Do you mind, or will that make your head hurt?

BRAD. Huh? Oh – no I'm ok.

(**LINDA** *puts on "In the Bush" by Musique.)*

CONNIE. Are you a good dancer?

BRAD. *(shy)* I don't know.

CONNIE. What's your favorite dance?

BRAD. The Hustle.

LINDA. I like the funky chicken. *(self punishing)* I mean I used to like it when it was in style, now it's out of date.

CONNIE. *(following* **LINDA***'s lead)* Yeah.

(The music plays – it has that scratchy album quality.)

LINDA. Do you like this? It isn't new – it's an old song. I like their old songs, do you like the Bee Gees?

CONNIE. I didn't know you liked them, you never tell me anything, what's the big secret.

LINDA. There's no secret, I have all their albums.

CONNIE. *(low grade despair)* Why don't you ever teach me new dances?

LINDA. What? I don't know any new dances.

CONNIE. You were doing new dances last night at the party. *(to* **BRAD***)* She's a great dancer.

BRAD. *(being polite)* I'd love to see your moves.

CONNIE. You were dancing with everyone, and you were doing these moves and you were all:

(She gets up and approximates the dance **LINDA** *did. It's old school disco.)*

LINDA. Oh
No it goes

(She does it.)

CONNIE. Oh

*(***LINDA** *continues to demonstrate.)*

Oh right

LINDA. And then

*(***LINDA** *does another move.)*

CONNIE. And there was something like…

*(***CONNIE** *tries to do a move.)*

LINDA. You mean this?

*(***LINDA** *shows her,* **CONNIE** *tries to do it.)*

*(***BRAD** *watches for a while.)*

BRAD. *(shy)* Do you know this?

(He shows them a new dance.)

(They try it.)

You have to swing it like this.

*(***CONNIE***'s doing it wrong.)*

No no, you go like this.

*(***CONNIE** *keeps trying.)*

No, look:

(**CONNIE** *gives up and just does her own version.* **LINDA**'*s doing it.*)

LINDA. That's so cute. You know what this reminds me of? *(she starts doing another move)* You know what I'm talking about?

BRAD. Yeah yeah yeah *(he cracks up)*

(**BRAD** *and* **LINDA** *are doing* **LINDA**'*s moves.* **CONNIE** *is getting frustrated but keeps trying.*)

(**CONNIE** *starts freestyling. They laugh. They all take turns freestyling. The moves get more elaborate and intense. It escalates until it is almost a competition, a bacchanal. It's both enjoyable and a little insane.*)

(Eventually they're worn out – they laugh and clap and stop dancing. **LINDA** *takes the needle off the record.)*

(to **LINDA***)* That was fun. You're pretty good

LINDA. *(smiles politely)* No I'm not

BRAD. Well I // thought –

LINDA. *(smile drops)* I don't care what you think, I don't know you.

CONNIE. She hates men.

BRAD. Oh, so //

LINDA. I'M NOT A DYKE *(smiles politely)* I'm sorry – I'm – *(to* **CONNIE***) And you're the one who hates men Connie //*

CONNIE. I like them but as pawns.

LINDA. I just don't like cruelty of any kind that's all //

CONNIE. Then you don't like men of any kind //

LINDA. That's not a *sine qua non* Connie //

CONNIE. *(dancing)* Hooa hooa

BRAD. I hope you don't think I was being cruel just now // I was just

CONNIE. *(inventing things)* You're looking at my breasts.

BRAD. What?

LINDA. She's –

CONNIE. Am I just breasts to you?

BRAD. I // didn't

CONNIE. *(sublimated anger)* Just forget it Do you want a black coffee or something? //

LINDA. Are you from around here? Or //

BRAD. I'm from Kansas. I got out of Vietnam about a year ago.

LINDA. *(delicately)* Oh…

BRAD. I've been floating around a little bit.

CONNIE. *(cheerful)* I've never been to Vietnam, was it nice?

LINDA. Connie, he was in a *war*!

CONNIE. *(grumpy)* You're always so *negative*!

LINDA. *(ignoring her)* What made you come to LA, Brad?

BRAD. I'm thinking more about my future.

LINDA. Future's important.

BRAD. I don't want to focus on anything but my career.

LINDA. Do you have a girlfriend?

BRAD. I just want to focus on my career.

CONNIE. What do you do?

BRAD. I'm a chef.

LINDA. Really?

BRAD. Well I'm in training, I'm at the French institute.

CONNIE. The French institute That's like a really good school // right?

LINDA. I like *coq au vin* Can you make // that?

CONNIE. I like rich foods //

LINDA. Me too, creams // butters

CONNIE. (But sometimes I like a plain plate of steamed kale) //

LINDA. I like to eat, sometimes I eat compulsively, no I'm kidding HA HA HA HA (no but I do) *I used to be bone thin* //

CONNIE. *You're not fat!*

LINDA. *(slightly hysterical)* Connie you have to remember to put the ad in the // chronicle

CONNIE. *I told you I put the article in already I put it in a hundred times*! //

LINDA. *(anxious)* Why isn't anyone responding? How are we gonna make rent?

BRAD. Are you looking for a roommate ?

LINDA. *(excited)* Why, do you know anyone?

BRAD. Well – I might be looking for a place.

CONNIE. You're a guy!

LINDA. He could have his own room.

CONNIE. Why can't you just stay at Terry's, his pad is blazin!

BRAD. He – he asked me to move. He needs more space.

LINDA. *(eye roll)* Terry's such a Casanova, he's always on the make.

BRAD. Anyway it was just temporary //

LINDA. *(manic, defensive) This is only temporary too* I'll probably be getting my own place soon, or if I'm in a relationship we'll move in together //

CONNIE. *(worried)* You're not gonna try to get it on with me are you? because I was almost raped in Venice Beach once //

BRAD. *(surprised)* Oh my god – //

CONNIE. Stop staring at my breasts //

LINDA. *(mollifying)* Connie, I get a good vibe off him.

CONNIE. *(to* **BRAD**, *a threat)* I took classes in La Jolla, I could knife you.

BRAD. I guess I could look for a place in West Hollywood.

LINDA. *(to* **CONNIE***)* See, everyone wants to live in West Hollywood!

CONNIE. *(to* **BRAD***)* Alright you can live here but I might knife you maybe.

BRAD. So…we're *roommates*?

LINDA. That's your room There's a bed and a dresser //

CONNIE. We're not giving you a blanket or sheets You need your own.

BRAD. How much is rent? //

CONNIE. Eighty one dollars and you owe from last month too so can you pay that?

BRAD. Do you think you could lend me some clothes //

CONNIE. "LIMBO, LIMBO" //

LINDA. *(pointing to her nightshirt)* Something like this?

BRAD. Uhhhh ha ha, no, I – I // can't

LINDA. Well you can't wear a towel!

(The doorbell rings.)

BRAD. Maybe that's Terry!

*(***LINDA** *crosses to the door, looks through the peephole.)*

LINDA. *(loud whisper)* It's Mrs. *Wicker!*

BRAD. Who? //

(Doorbell rings.)

CONNIE. Get in here and put something on!

(She rushes **BRAD** *into the bedroom and slams the door.)*

I'm gonna climb down the fire escape and find Terry!

LINDA. Just go out the front door!

CONNIE. *(dizzy)* I thought that would be conspicuous!

(She exits hurriedly through the kitchen door.)

LINDA. *(exasperated) Connie, where are you going!?*

(She returns, attempting to rush but unsure where. She vaguely bops around in circles.)

CONNIE. *(worried) I don't know where to go!!*

*(***BRAD** *opens the bedroom door:)*

BRAD. *(whisper)* Come in here with me!!

(Doorbell rings a bunch of times.)

*(***CONNIE** *rushes towards the bedroom, but then stops short and goes back into the kitchen.)*

LINDA. *Connie!!!*

*(**CONNIE** rushes back instantly with a large knife. She enters the bedroom. **LINDA** answers the door, **MRS. WICKER** makes a beeline for the sofa.)*

MRS. WICKER. There's gum on that.

LINDA. Oh that – that's // just

MRS. WICKER. Watch it You might lose your security deposit //

LINDA. Do you want a cup of coffee?

MRS. WICKER. *(prickly)* Coffee is too acidulous for my stomach.

LINDA. Tea? //

MRS. WICKER. You're late with rent //

LINDA. So how's everything goin?

MRS. WICKER. Fine I don't know How are you ?

LINDA. I //

MRS. WICKER. *(anxious)* I have to throw a shower for my niece!

LINDA. That's nice.

MRS. WICKER. Maybe you give parties but I don't so I'm having a hard time!

LINDA. It's not that // hard.

MRS. WICKER. I feel like I do everything wrong //

LINDA. *(trying to brighten things)* What's your niece's name //

MRS. WICKER. *(suspicious) Why do you need to know that!?*

(STOP)

LINDA. What do you mean? //

MRS. WICKER. *(softening)* I'm sorry It's Betty //

LINDA. Betty: Is she that newscaster you // were

MRS. WICKER. No that's my other niece Her name is Tania She won a Peabody award. *(beat)* I'm sorry for yelling at you before //

LINDA. You didn't // yell

MRS. WICKER. *(yelling) YES-I-DID! (penitent)* I'm just anxious //

LINDA. Why are you // anxious

MRS. WICKER. *(hostile) I told you I'm giving a party for my NIECE!*

LINDA. *(a beat)* I could – help you // if you

MRS. WICKER. Thank you but I don't want people to treat me like an invalid.

LINDA. You're not an // invalid

MRS. WICKER. But people treat me that way //

LINDA. I've never seen people treat you // that way

MRS. WICKER. Are you the measure of all things?

LINDA. *(beat)* I'm sure you'd make a very nice party // for your

MRS. WICKER. It's a *shower* not a *party*.

LINDA. Uh... Do you want some tea? //

MRS. WICKER. *(a bit hysterical) I'd love some!*

LINDA. We have Lapsang Souchon //

MRS. WICKER. *That's my favorite tea*!

LINDA. *(jolted)* I. I got it, as. A gift // from

MRS. WICKER. *(as* **LINDA** *pours tea)* It's my favorite that tea Lapsang Souchon Oh thank you Linda Oh I love the balls I didn't know you had these Anyways I'm sorry for yelling //

LINDA. You // didn't

MRS. WICKER. OW DAMMIT IT'S HOT //

LINDA. Blow on it //

MRS. WICKER. *(casual at first, then increasingly terrified and real)*: It's just I'm anxious *all* the time not just about my niece's party although I'm scared to call the person to do the calligraphy for the invitations?

LINDA. Oh but that's ridiculous // I'll

MRS. WICKER. Well maybe to you its ridiculous to me it's a nightmare, but that's a whole other thing, I'm just anxious Ha ha ha OH this is delicious It's very hot //

LINDA. Why are you // so anxious

MRS. WICKER. OW I burnt my tongue! Ha ha ha *(austere)* but no I'm just *anxious* all the time *(jovial)* hey did you guys paint in here?

LINDA. No //

MRS. WICKER. It looks great //

LINDA. It's the same stucco //

MRS. WICKER. Stucco is so practical isn't it? And it brings the room into three dimensions //

LINDA. The room is *in* three // dimensions

MRS. WICKER. Some people think there are four dimensions or five or an infinite amount of dimensions And some people think we live inside a hologram *That makes me anxious*!

LINDA. Have you ever considered medication? //

MRS. WICKER. No.

LINDA. My friend says it helps //

MRS. WICKER. Well I'm on medication and it doesn't.

LINDA. You just said you weren't on //it

MRS. WICKER. *(simmering)* No-I-said-I-never-*considered*-it-which-is-true-because-it-was-prescribed-for-me-and-I-don't-TAKE-IT!

(STOP)

LINDA. My friend Faye // says

MRS. WICKER. *(curious)* Who's-Faye?

LINDA. She's my // friend

MRS. WICKER. *(resentful) I don't know Faye!*

LINDA. She works with me in the flower shop //

MRS. WICKER. *(indictment) You don't work in a flower shop!*

LINDA. No, I – I *do.*

MRS. WICKER. Really So why aren't there any flowers around?

LINDA. We have these:

(produces flowers)

MRS. WICKER. These are fake! See: *(She pulls off a petal)* oh Sorry.

LINDA. Those were expensive.

MRS. WICKER. *(ashamed, mortified)* Oh. I – I didn't //

LINDA. Well it's sort of dying anyways // so

MRS. WICKER. *(defensive)* THEN HERE, JUST TAKE TEN BUCKS!!!!

(She rushes to her purse.)

Sometimes I mistake real things for fake things. *(she looks* **LINDA** *up and down)* And vice versa.

(Hands her some dough.)

LINDA. I can't take your money //

MRS. WICKER. Why not I can take yours Except you never pay your *rent* so I *DON'T.*

LINDA. Sometimes we get behind // but

MRS. WICKER. Yes I told Henry that but his patience is wearing thin //

LINDA. But we're planning // to

MRS. WICKER. *(gets up to go)* Anyway I have to go hook a rug now Bye //

LINDA. Mrs. Wicker I'm – *worried* about you.

(pause)

MRS. WICKER. You don't even like me.

LINDA. I like you.

(She turns to **LINDA.***)*

MRS. WICKER. *(still slightly suspicious)* Well…that's very sweet of you.

(short pause)

LINDA. My friend Faye // has

MRS. WICKER. *(excited) How's Faye*?!?

LINDA. She's fine, she has a problem similar to yours //

MRS. WICKER. *(bitter recrimination) I don't have a problem!*

LINDA. Her medication helps her. She used to get anxious but // she's

MRS. WICKER. *(nervous)* Ok but don't talk about it because that brings on the panic attack!

LINDA. Do you have the medication on you?

MRS. WICKER. *(beseeching)* No I'm scared to take it I don't know what's in those pills!!

LINDA. What's the // matter?

MRS. WICKER. I-can't-breathe //

LINDA. Sit down Let me get you // a glass of

MRS. WICKER. *(real fear)* My doctor says if I don't take my pills I'll have a complete *breakdown.*

LINDA. Well...can't you just – take them?

MRS. WICKER: *(rage) No I can't "just take them"!*

(We hear **BRAD** *and* **CONNIE** *arguing from OS, loud stage whispers:)*

CONNIE. *(os)* Brad, we *have* to get it on.

BRAD. *(os)* But it's so tiny…

CONNIE. *(os)* Really? It's too big for me. But I guess for a man it's different.

BRAD. *(os)* Can we get it to fit?

(A few small, strange noises. **MRS WICKER***'s eyes widen.)*

MRS. WICKER. Who's *that?*

LINDA. *(shrugs)* I don't hear anything.

BRAD. *(os)* Connie it's too *tight.* We'll never get it on.

CONNIE. *(os)* I'm trying to stretch it out.

MRS. WICKER. You don't hear that?

LINDA. I can't hear anything. But I'm half deaf.

MRS. WICKER. What do you mean?

LINDA. I'm deaf in my left ear I had scarlet fever as a child //

MRS. WICKER. I had scarlet fever too but my mother gave me a milk bath Did your mother give you a milk bath? //

LINDA. I think Michael Jackson gives himself milk baths //

MRS. WICKER. I think he's a better dancer than Fred Astaire! //

CONNIE. *(os)* JUST HOLD STILL! I AM TRYING TO STRETCH IT OVER // YOU.

LINDA. I love "Off the Wall," it's a great // album!

BRAD. *(os)* It's all puffy now! Does it look weird?

CONNIE. *(os)* Forget about how it looks, how does it *feel*??

(**MRS. WICKER** *stands, horrified.)*

BRAD. *(os)* Silky!

(**MRS. WICKER** *looks around trying to ascertain where the voices are coming from, walks slowly to bedroom.)*

LINDA. Mrs. Wicker!!

CONNIE. *(os)* See? I knew we could get it on!

(**MRS. WICKER** *opens the door to the bedroom.)*

(**BRAD** *is standing in the doorway in a frilly nightgown, caught.)*

BRAD. *(sheepish)* Hiee.

LINDA. *("acting natural")* This is my friend Brad.

(**CONNIE** *enters, casually holding the kitchen knife.)*

MRS. WICKER. Nice getup. You girls are really cookin with gas. //

CONNIE. *(nonchalant)* Hey Mrs Wicker.

LINDA. *(to* **MRS. WICKER***)* Brad is a transvestite.

CONNIE. We want him to be our new roommate.

BRAD. I'm not a // transvestite.

MRS. WICKER. *(to* **BRAD***)* I read about you in magazines, I mean about people who share your lifestyle.

BRAD. I'm not a *transvestite.*

LINDA. *(eyeballing* **BRAD***)* Yes you *are.*

MRS. WICKER. Transvestites are always pretending to be something they're not, they pretend to be women and they pretend to be not-transvestites and they just live in a world of pretend!

BRAD. But // I'm

MRS. WICKER. *(reverie)* But I like to pretend When I was a girl I used to pretend all the time but then my reality would shatter and that's how my anxiety attacks started!

CONNIE. You have anxiety attacks? //

MRS. WICKER. *(innocently)* No.

CONNIE. But you just // said

MRS. WICKER. *(unfettered rage)* BUT I WAS PRETENDING DIDN'T YOU HEAR A GODDAM WORD I SAID *(conversational to* **BRAD***)* Do you feel trapped in your body because I feel trapped in my body Is that how you feel? //

BRAD. Uh //

MRS. WICKER. A lot of the ancient philosophers believed that the body is a prison for the soul //

CONNIE. I don't believe in souls!

LINDA. Mrs. Wicker: we would like Brad to be our roommate.

MRS. WICKER. But he's a man! *(eyeing him)* Well sort of.

CONNIE. He's gay. That's practically a woman!

MRS. WICKER. *(a fun caper:)* Well I guess that's alright but you have to ask Henry. But I like fags My hairdresser is a faggot. *(to* **BRAD***)* Do you tell any good jokes because my hairdresser is quite a joker He should be on television that's how funny he is. HA HA HA. *(to* **LINDA***)* I'm starting to feel relaxed, I think gays relax me.

*(***BRAD** *trips on the rug on his way to sitting down.)*

BRAD. Whoops –

CONNIE. Brad! //

MRS. WICKER. You're a crack-up!

LINDA. Are you ok?

BRAD. *(rubbing his jaw)* Just a nick //

MRS. WICKER. I saw a movie where a kid kept falling down, I think he was in Russia, I think he was in a gulag, I like all these weird kind of movies, I have very esoteric tastes.

LINDA. Brad is going to sleep in Beverly's old room.

MRS. WICKER. Oh, old Bev, what happened to her?

LINDA. She got married.

MRS. WICKER. Oh the poor bitch HA HA HA. Did she move out?

CONNIE. Just yesterday, she went on her honeymoon.

MRS. WICKER. Where, San Quentin? HA HA HA HA. I don't know why I'm laughing. HA HA HA HA HA. *(to* **BRAD***)* Do you like Russian movies?

CONNIE. I don't like foreign films.

MRS. WICKER. They play them over at that art house theatre on Fairfax. *(she eats a triscuit, happier now)* I feel very relaxed by gays.

(doorbell rings)

CONNIE. I'll get it.

(She opens the door and **TERRY** *enters.)*

Terry where the hell've // you been

BRAD. Where are my *clothes*?

TERRY. *(to* **BRAD***)* Dude what happened to you, I figured you passed out "Oh hey Mrs. Wicker" //

MRS. WICKER. Who are you? //

*(***TERRY** *produces wallet.)*

TERRY. I'm // in –

MRS. WICKER. Did you pay your rent //

BRAD. My wallet! //

TERRY. And the money's all there you can count it (Except for ten bucks I ran outta gas) Nice nightie by the way //

BRAD. *(to* **TERRY***) Where are my clothes?*

TERRY. You played a game of strip poker You must've been really hammered.

BRAD. *(to* **TERRY***)* Do me a solid and bring my suitcase down?

TERRY. Down where?

LINDA. Brad's moving in.

TERRY. He's *what?*

CONNIE. He's our new roommate! //

TERRY. You *dog* //

MRS. WICKER. *(correcting)* He's not a dog He's a faggot.

TERRY. *(laughing)* He's *what?*

*(***CONNIE** *whispers furtively in* **TERRY***'s ear.)*

BRAD. Listen I'm gonna take a shower is that okay? *(to* **TERRY***)* Would you mind bringing down // my

TERRY. Alright alright –

*(***BRAD** *exits for the shower)*

LINDA. You can use my body bar //

CONNIE. The showerhead isn't working you have to twist it //

LINDA. I thought Wicker fixed it //

CONNIE. (He-did-and-then-it-broke)

BRAD. *(to* **MRS. WICKER***)* Nice meeting you.

*(***MRS. WICKER** *just looks at him.* **BRAD** *exits to bathroom.* **TERRY** *opens the door,* **MR. WICKER** *enters as he's leaving.)*

WICKER. You kids wanted me to fix that faucet //

TERRY. (Hi-mr-Wicker-bye-mr-Wicker*)* //

MRS. WICKER. Henry, oh, sing "my way" //

WICKER. She likes my pipes.

CONNIE. Are you a good singer //

WICKER. *(sings, holding his toolbelt)* "Regrets –

MRS. WICKER. (That's-enough-I-have-a-headache)

CONNIE. *(to* **MR. WICKER***)* Are // you

MRS. WICKER. (You kids have any Aspirin?)

WICKER. *(to* **MRS. WICKER***)* One day I'll be dead and I won't be able to sing to you.

MRS. WICKER. *(weirdly flirtatious)* Don't tease! and anyways, I plan on committing suicide in a few days, so I'll be dead first. Ha ha ha. *LADIES FIRST. No seriously, I want to die.* NO I'M KIDDING. *(her smile disintegrating here) No it's not funny.* I know I'm naughty *(she yawns)* Ok bye.

(She exits. It's just **LINDA, CONNIE** *and* **WICKER.** *It's awkward. We hear the shower starting up in the bathroom, very faint.)*

CONNIE. *(bolts up)* Well
I have to go

WICKER. To – //

CONNIE. *(improvising)* The-beach-I-have-to-surf.

*(***CONNIE** *produces a large surfboard, exits.* **WICKER** *and* **LINDA** *have a moment.)*

LINDA. I'm. Uh…going too.

WICKER. Where are you off to?

LINDA. I'm gonna read my book.

(beat)

WICKER. Book huh? You're a regular librarian.

LINDA. *(casual)* I'm researching new apartment options for myself.

WICKER. New apartment? Hey, you got a contract, you're not goin anywhere!

LINDA. Not right now, but soon. I can't stay here forever! I'm still young. I have a whole future ahead of me.

WICKER. Oh yeah?

LINDA. This was always just temporary, I'll need my own place soon.

WICKER. Where you gonna move?

LINDA. West Hollywood. There's a lot of shops there //

WICKER. Yeah and there's a lot of *fags* there!

LINDA. *(momentarily thwarted)* Well I'll just ignore them! *(softening)* Or I might just move in with my boyfriend, I have to see.

WICKER. I didn't know you had a boyfriend.

(beat)

LINDA. Well, I do. He's – I mean it's still very new // but

WICKER. *Hey,* how do you fit four fags on a barstool? //

LINDA. What – I – I don't // know.

WICKER. Flip it over! Ha ha ha ha.

*(**LINDA** smiles politely, maybe forces a tiny chuckle. **WICKER** looks at her, his smile fades. Pause. He fidgets nervously with his toolbelt.)*

I'll miss ya. You know, when you go.

LINDA. *(smiling sadly)* Yeah, right. Nobody misses me.

(a beat)

*(**LINDA** looks at him.)*

I told you I'm not doing this anymore.

(He sticks his hand down her pants.)

I told you // I

*(She quietly has an orgasm. It sounds a little like crying. He takes his hand out of her pants. **LINDA** stands there, tears well up in her eyes.)*

(He kisses her paternally on the head. He means well. We hear the shower turn off in the bathroom.)

(vulnerable) Do you think I'm… *(pause; affectless)* Forget it.

(Doorbell rings. Awkward pause. Doorbell rings.)

WICKER. You gonna get that?

(doorbell rings)

*(**WICKER** opens the door.)*

*(It's **TERRY**. He brings a suitcase in with him.)*

(re: suitcase) What the hell is that, you movin in?

TERRY. I just brought Brad's stuff – *hey* Linda –

*(**LINDA** shakily goes to her room. She quietly shuts the door and locks it – loudly.)*

*(to **WICKER**)* Like this.

*(He twists two fingers together, indicating his tight relationship with **LINDA**.)*

WICKER. Who's Brad?

TERRY. Linda and Connie's new roommate – didn't // they

WICKER. Linda and Connie's WHAT???!

TERRY. Well – he's –

*(**BRAD** enters from the bathroom, wearing that frilly thing **CONNIE** has lent him.)*

BRAD. Hey, Ter, thanks a ton –

TERRY. Brad –

BRAD. Oh and you must be Mr. Wicker, good to meet you, I'm Brad.

*(**BRAD** extends a hand to shake **WICKER**'s. **WICKER** stares at him.)*

WICKER. *(eyeing him)* Oh.

I see.

Heh heh heh.

*(**WICKER** cruelly extends a limp wrist, smiling. **BRAD** retracts his hand.)*

So you're the new *(makes quotation marks with his finger)* "roommate"

BRAD. Yeah // I'm

WICKER. Uh-huh.

(beat)

Uh-huh

(beat)

ah ha ha ha ha,

(beat)

AH AHA HA HA HA

(He eyeballs **BRAD**, *looks him up and down, shakes his head, smiling impishly.)*

And what do you. uh. "do" – for a "living"?

BRAD. I'm a cook.

WICKER. A *cook.*

BRAD. Well I'm training.

WICKER. That's not code for hustler is it?

BRAD. No – oh, no, me? no I'm //

TERRY. Brad's a good guy.

WICKER. How do you know?

TERRY. Brad was in Nam, he's a serviceman.

BRAD. I was a cook.

WICKER. A cook huh? You two ever
"cook" together?
HA HA HA HA HA
Maybe you could teach my wife to "cook".

*(***TERRY** *rifles few a through albums over the following – he puts a record on.)*

BRAD. Well. Okay. I –

WICKER. If you could only get pregnant I'd have you barefoot and in my kitchen in no time.

BRAD. [*not knowing how to take any of this*] Uh.

WICKER. [*private joke that no one understands*] Heh heh heh heh

TERRY. Brad can't *get* pregnant!

WICKER. *(to* **TERRY***)* And I'm sure you tried.

(He bats his eyelashes at **TERRY***.)*

Anyways see you pussies later I got a date with a shower nozzle.

(**WICKER** *exits to bathroom with his toolkit. Music starts: Giorgio Moroder's "Knights in White Satin.")*

BRAD. What a jerk.

TERRY. Wicker, nah, he's ok.

(**TERRY** *checks out the album cover, feeling the funk. This goes on for a bit.)*

Y'know Brad, I'm kinda mad at you.

BRAD. What?

TERRY. I dunno. I thought you and me were gonna be roomies. I mean I don't wanna get all pussy about it but I thought it was going pretty good with us.

(**BRAD** *gets a little stolid, a little chilly.)*

BRAD. Yeah well… This is just cheaper – with school and everything. I could use the extra bread.

TERRY. Well you couldda said something…gimme some kinda "advanced notice" over here.

BRAD. *(softening)* I guess I felt like I was getting in the way… with all your chicks and everything.

TERRY. *(hurt)* Gettin in the way? Dude, you're like my best friend.

(**BRAD** *looks at him, tries to determine if he's being teased.)*

BRAD. *(macho, joking)* Shut the fuck up.

TERRY. What, I'm serious!

BRAD. *(overcompensating)* Don't be such a girl.

TERRY. *Whoa,* I'm not the one wearing ladies underpants you fuckin freak!

(**TERRY** *pushes him,* **BRAD** *hits* **TERRY** *back.)*

(almost a come on) You gonna start with me? Huh?

BRAD. Get the fuck off me.

TERRY. Make me, faggot.

*(**TERRY** straddles him, **BRAD** is laughing hysterically, his arms pinned to the sofa. It's rough but still playful.)*

BRAD. *(laughing)* Fuck you! Get off me!

*(He slaps **BRAD** lightly in the face. **BRAD** laughs hysterically. **TERRY** imitates him laughing.)*

*(**TERRY** thrusts a few times to the music, fake-moaning. **BRAD** looks at him, trying not to give anything away. **TERRY** bolts up, distracted.)*

TERRY. *Shit,* it was Felicia right? She kept you up? That's what this is about //

BRAD. Who?

TERRY. The screamer.

BRAD. *(cockblocked)* Oh – yeah //

TERRY. I stuffed a sock in her mouth to shut her up but then she got it all foamy and had some kinda seizure. *(sad)* Skank. That was my good sock too. *(pause)* Dude, what's a matter?

BRAD. What?

(pause)

TERRY. You look like you're gonna cry.

BRAD. *(defensive smile)* Shut the fuck up...

TERRY. Don't tell me you're getting all sensitive on me, witcha new "lifestyle"? Huh faggot? HA HA HA.

BRAD. Your mama!

*(**BRAD** smacks **TERRY** on the ass. **TERRY** smacks him back. Smack, smack, back and forth. **TERRY** dances a little, sidles up to **BRAD**, kinda homoerotic.)*

TERRY. *(mock eroticism)* Yeah you like that you little faggot huh? You like it when I slap your ass? HEH HEH HEH

*(**TERRY** examines his cuticles, drops the game.)*

(contemplative) Dude: I burst a blood vessel in my penis last night. Karen has an overbite. Bitch.

(pause)

BRAD. *(duly humiliated)* I gotta do some work now.

TERRY. Ooh, listen to this: This shit's blazin. Hooa hooa.

*(**TERRY** turns it up a little bit, checks himself out in the mirror. He fingers the chain around his neck, dances a little to the music, maybe lipsynchs a bit. **BRAD** stares, filled with longing. **TERRY** unbuttons a few more buttons from his shirt while he dances – he's <u>very serious</u>.)*

So what are you up to tonight? Karen has this totally foxy cousin I thought we // could

BRAD. Who's Karen

TERRY. A fox, this foxy girl, I met her in Pasadena.

BRAD. No, no chicks –

TERRY. You never do shit with me anymore!

BRAD. I have to practice //

TERRY. Practice cunnilingus on Karen's cousin!

BRAD. Funny.

TERRY. You been in L.A. how long now, four five months? When was the last time you got laid?

BRAD. What about Cynthia?

TERRY. Chick from St Louis? I thought you were just friends.

BRAD. We were, before I fucked her.

TERRY. My man!

(They slap each other five.)

BRAD. I gotta do some work.

TERRY. It's Saturday night.

BRAD. I'm in *cooking* school –

TERRY. Oh yeah? whatchu cookin up, a *sandwich?!?*

(He gestures towards the girls rooms, he laughs.)

BRAD. Cmon.

TERRY. Whaddaya mean "cmon" That's some smokin snatch in there!

BRAD. It's not like that.

TERRY. Yeah I'll *bet.*

BRAD. Anyway it's degrading to talk about girls like that.

TERRY. Nah they like that shit.

(**BRAD** *forces a tiny smile. He looks very unhappy.)*

What the fuck is wrong with you man, you're actin all weird.

BRAD. I. Uh. I'm tired – from the move.

TERRY. Dude, you moved a suitcase two flights down the stairs! And Karen's cousin has breasts like *pendulums!*

(**BRAD** *gets a bit interior. No response.)*

Dude?

BRAD. Do you ever…

(pause)

TERRY. What's a matter?

BRAD. Do you…

Do you ever feel…

Like…

empty?

(**TERRY** *considers this briefly.)*

TERRY. *(quizzically)* You mean like hungry?

BRAD. No

I mean…

Inside.

(silence)

TERRY. *(sincere)* Inside where?

(STOP; then playfully, fobbing it off)

You're such a little *faggot*

(slaps his knee, as if speaking to a dog) "Cmere faggot"

(He starts play-boxing with **BRAD** *who ineptly tries to defend himself, and sort of fobs it off, smiling.)*

BRAD. Stop it.

TERRY. *(having fun)* "Stop it"

*(***TERRY*** punches him. It hurts, and* **BRAD** *tries to laugh it off)*

*(***TERRY*** jabs, jabs, jabs.* **TERRY** *blocks* **BRAD** *wherever he turns, he's outwardly "playful" – but relentless – he jabs)*

BRAD. I gotta put on some clothes –

(He hits **BRAD**. **BRAD** *hits him back – aiming to hurt him enough to shut him down.)*

TERRY. You call that a punch?
That's a sucka punch cocksucka I'm Joe Frazier

(He jabs.)

"I'm Muhammed Ali"

(He jabs.)

I am the gray-test!

*(***TERRY***, overadrenalized, hits* **BRAD** *square on the face.)*

BRAD. *(covering his nose)* JESUS.

TERRY. *(laughing at him)* Don't pussy out on me.

(There's blood on his finger.)

BRAD. I'm gonna get some ice.

TERRY. *(takes needle off record, goes o.s.)* Nah lemme get it, is it broken?

BRAD. *(quiet, looks at himself in the mirror)* Terry, what the hell's your problem!

TERRY. *(os)* Chicks dig blood, it's cool. *(reenters)* You're all out; they must have used it up at the party.

BRAD. Well get me some uh, some *tissues* // or something

TERRY. Alright alright put your head up.

*(***TERRY** *sits him down,* **BRAD** *puts his head up.* **TERRY** *produces a wad of tissues to stop the bleeding.)*

So what should I tell Tina?

BRAD. *(with tissues up his nose)* Who?

TERRY. KAREN'S COUSIN!!

BRAD. I have homework.

TERRY. "homework"

BRAD. Yeah "homework" I have to make pie crusts //

TERRY. Why make crusts when you can have the whole pie? //

BRAD. Terry –

TERRY. She has eraser-nips //

BRAD. Good-night Terry.

*(***BRAD** *pushes* **TERRY** *to the door.)*

TERRY. I'll be at the Rolley Pony if you change your –

*(***BRAD** *slams the door.)*

(Lies for a moment against the door.)

(Wipes the blood from his nose.)

(Looks at himself in the mirror, deeply sad.)

(Suddenly he bounces away – shakes this off.)

(Shakes his arms out. Jogs in place, shadow boxes. Looks at the frilly nightgown he's wearing, rolls his eyes with disgust.)

(Phone rings. **BRAD** *answers it.)*

BRAD. *(into phone)* Hello,
Who's calling? Sure hold on
"Linda?"

(beat)

"LINDA?"

(beat)

(Slowly, the doorknob to her room turns.)

*(*LINDA*, somewhat zombified, opens the door.)*

(She looks like hell. Mascara runs down her face, eyes bleary.)

LINDA. *(hoarsely, looks into the distance)* What.

BRAD. Todd Stengler is on the phone –

(She grabs the phone from him violently.)

I should go change…

*(*BRAD *exits.* LINDA *smiles, tries to calm down, steady her breathing; it's a bit mad. She picks up the phone.)*

LINDA. Todd. Hi.

Our what?

Date?

(She could just die.)

W-w-w-what date?

(covering hysterically)

No-I-wasn't-drunk-I-remember

I mean-I'm-not-a-drunk HA HA HA

(Beat; then shutting her eyes, as if it's a dream)

Dancing no I love to dance

(She opens her eyes, sees her reflection in the mirror. Oops, she's "fat and ugly" – remember, LINDA*? Her smile crumples.)*

Oh but.

I can't

(beat)

Because

I can't…

(She tries to hide the deflation in her voice.)

(She has enormous trouble getting the next lines out.)

'Cause I. I don't feel well

(This is killing her.)

I just don't feel well
I know I'm
I just
I'm sorry I don't
I don't feel well

(As she speaks the energy leaks out of her until she can barely move or say anything.)

(She slowly hangs up, expressionless, her grip still on the receiver, her eyes closed.)

(This goes on for a bit.)

(Then)

(She releases her grip.)

(She winds her way to the bar.)

(She gets a glass, pours herself a drink.)

(Takes a sip.)

(She makes her way to the record player.)

(Shifts the needle. It's Giorgio Moroder's "Chase")

(She closes her eyes, feels the music.)

(She goes to the sofa, drink in hand.)

(She waits.)

(Music builds. Lights dim.)

2.

(The record skips; no music, just scratches.)

(Later that day. Early evening – a swath of light against the curtains, beginning of sunset. The living room is empty.)

(Doorbell rings. No answer.)

(Doorbell rings.)

(Doorbell rings.)

BRAD. *(os)* "Just a minute"

*(**BRAD** enters, crosses to door. He's got a bandage on his nose. He's wearing a skin tight patchwork denim number, flared pants, matching jacket, no shirt underneath. On his way to the door he trips and falls flat on his face.)*

OW.

(Gets up. Feels his cheek. Slight bruising.)

Ow.

*(Sees the record skipping – removes the needle. Doorbell rings. He opens the door. **CONNIE** enters with a surfboard. Her hair is wet.)*

Hey Connie //

CONNIE. Sorry Brad, I left my key here by accident – don't tell Linda, she thinks I'm irresponsible.

BRAD. I didn't know you liked to surf.

CONNIE. I feel like the water gets bad energy off me.

BRAD. Did you have a good time?

CONNIE. I met a girl on the beach, her name's Mandy, we were both in *Miracle Worker,* isn't that neat? Our fathers are both ministers.

BRAD. I didn't know your dad's a minister.

CONNIE. *(puts away her stuff)* I'm very religious. Where's my rosary? Oh it doesn't matter, I think the beads all fell off. I don't think I really believe in anything anymore frankly. Where's my wax?

BRAD. Your what?

CONNIE. For my –? oh here.

(She waxes her surfboard.)

Maybe I never believed in anything. I mean I was very deceitful as a little girl, but we were poor. That made it all worth it.

*(**BRAD**'s confused but tries to brush it off.)*

BRAD. Uh, you got some messages, Sam in 6G and Steve in 8F –

CONNIE. *Brad!* What happened to your face? You're hurt!

(She goes over to him.)

BRAD. What? Oh – I uh – I fell.

CONNIE. You're very accident-prone. Did you put ice on it?

BRAD. Oh – yeah, I'm fine.

CONNIE. Let me see…

(She goes over to him and checks the bruise on his face. He stands there for a bit.)

BRAD. Ow.

CONNIE. I just want to make sure nothing's broken. *(sad)* You break one thing and then everything breaks.

BRAD. So… Whatcha doing tonight?

CONNIE. Going to the Peter Frampton concert with George.

BRAD. Who's George? Is that your boyfriend?

CONNIE. I just met him on the sidewalk.

BRAD. *(confused)* Just now?

CONNIE. Yeah.

(She gets her mascara. **BRAD** *'s a little weirded out.)*

BRAD. You must really like Peter Frampton.

CONNIE. No, I just get lonely and needy. *(blithe)* Oh well, hope I don't get raped! *(she shrugs, reapplies mascara)* You have a hot date tonight?

BRAD. Nah, I have homework.

CONNIE. You always have homework.

BRAD. You've only known me a couple of hours.

CONNIE. That's what I'm saying! I should set you up with my friend Mandy. She has an excellent character. *(pops the mascara back into her bag; then chilly:)* Unfortunately her breasts are just normal sized so you probably wouldn't be interested //

*(***LINDA** *enters.)*

LINDA. Brad, who was at the door?

CONNIE. No-one!

LINDA. Connie, did you forget your key again?

CONNIE. *Stop putting your things on me Linda!*

LINDA. *You're the one putting your things on me!*

BRAD. Girls come on, no fighting.

CONNIE. I gotta go blow my hair, I have a date.

LINDA. With who?

CONNIE. I'm going to the Peter Frampton concert.

LINDA. That concert's been sold out for months…

CONNIE. I know.

LINDA. *(betrayed)* You don't even like Frampton!

CONNIE. I'm getting more into him!

LINDA. Connie, you know I've been dying to get tickets to that concert!

CONNIE. Don't make me feel guilty. It's just a date –

LINDA. You're always on dates. I hardly ever see you anymore.

CONNIE. I can't help if guys want to go out with me –

LINDA. Maybe you could help it if you'd stop wearing tight shirts and shaking your boobs everywhere!!

CONNIE. I don't shake my boobs everywhere!!

*(***LINDA** *shakes her boobs angrily, mocking* **CONNIE.***)*

LINDA. *(shaking them as she speaks)* "Hi, I'm Connie, wanna go the Peter Frampton Concert?"

*(***CONNIE** *makes mean faces at her and shakes her boobs in retaliation.)*

CONNIE. "Hi, I'm Linda, I – I think I'm… I'm like… I'm so…"

(She can't think of anything. This upsets her. She keeps shaking her boobs and making faces to mask her disappointment in herself. **LINDA** *laughs openly at her.)*

SHUT UP! //

LINDA. YOU // SHUT UP.

BRAD. Girls, alright, come on! Stop this! Enough fighting. Ok?

(He puts his arms around them. They all stand huddled uncomfortably for a bit.)

CONNIE. I wish Mandy was here, she's the only one who gets me.

LINDA. Who's *Mandy*?

CONNIE. Someone who doesn't emotionally abuse me every two seconds, that's who *Mandy* is! She's a quality person for your information!

*(***CONNIE** *exits in a huff to her room, turns back for a moment.)*

(quiet disdain) "Stalks with petals"

(She exits, slamming the door behind her. **LINDA** *sighs, pours herself a drink. She sits on the sofa, thumbs through a McCalls.)*

BRAD. You're all dressed up. *(beat)* Whatcha doing tonight?

LINDA. Staying home. I don't know.

BRAD. What about "Todd Stengler"?

(pause)

LINDA. He's not my type.

(She goes back to her McCalls. Then turns to **BRAD***, tentative.)*

There's a Japanese movie at the art house on Beverly Boulevard, it's – it's supposed to be really good. We could…go together…

BRAD. I can't, I – I have homework.

LINDA. *(deflating, perceives this as a rejection)* Oh. Right.

BRAD. Maybe Mrs. Wicker could go with you //

LINDA. *(overreacts)* Well I don't want to go with *her*!

BRAD. Ok well – then hang out with me.

LINDA. You're busy. *(pause)* Anyway I like being by myself.

(Pause, she stares out into space, depressive. **BRAD** *comes up from behind her, he's being cute.)*

BRAD. *(playfully)* Liiindaaaa?

(She doesn't look at him.)

Hey you wanna see my impression of a giraffe?

(He does an impression of a giraffe. **LINDA** *cracks a smile.)*

I do a good cat, too.

(He does. She laughs.)

Better?

*(***LINDA** *nods yes. She looks at him, lovingly.)*

(pause)

LINDA. Did you ever play Faces?

BRAD. What's Faces?

LINDA. *(excited)* Do you wanna play?

BRAD. Ok.

LINDA. *(all excited)* Ok, so you tell me a kind of face to make, you know like happy, sad, and then I have to make that face.

BRAD. I don't think I'm gonna be good at Faces.

LINDA. No no you will – you'll be great. Ok now so tell me a face.

*(**BRAD** just looks at her.)*

BRAD. I'm scared.

LINDA. No – *no* it's *fun.*

(pause)

BRAD. Ok. *(he thinks)* Elated.

(She tries to look elated. She's getting into character. She's getting into character. She's elated.)

That's actually really good.

LINDA. Ok, now you.

BRAD. Ok.

LINDA. Anxious.

BRAD. Oh god, that's hard. Ok. *(pause; he starts to smile involuntarily)* Ok wait: *(he clears his throat)* Ok:

*(**BRAD** looks anxious. **LINDA** laughs.)*

I told you I'm not good // at this.

LINDA. No no, I'm laughing because it's good.

BRAD. You're so full of shit.

LINDA. Give me another one.

BRAD. Ok. Carefree //

LINDA. Carefree, ok //

BRAD. Wait:

but with an undercurrent of fanaticism.

LINDA. That's really hard!

BRAD. Well I'm moving you up a notch.

LINDA. That's not fair!

Ok, wait:

(She does it. They both laugh.)

Ok. You ready?

BRAD. Uh huh.

LINDA. Indecision //

BRAD. Oh shit...

LINDA. With an undercurrent of..uh – I don't know. Wait hold on. *(beat) Terror.*

BRAD. Ok.

(He does it. **CONNIE** *enters, unseen, sees them playing.* **BRAD***'s face is kind of hysterical. They both break out with laughter.)*

CONNIE. *(genuine betrayal)* You're playing Faces without me? Thanks a lot.

LINDA. You hate playing Faces.

CONNIE. *(hurt)* Excuse me. Who was the one who fucking taught you how to play Faces in the first place?

LINDA. Beverly.

CONNIE. No, not Beverly, *me, I* taught you Faces, that's MY game.

LINDA. Maybe it's your game, but Beverly taught it to // me.

BRAD. Listen Connie, just play faces with us // ok?

CONNIE. No //

LINDA. Just play // Faces!

CONNIE. *(jumps onto the couch, makes herself instantly cozy)* Ok-give-me-a-face! //

BRAD. Ok...mania!

*(***CONNIE** *makes a manic face)*

LINDA. WITH AN UNDERCURRENT of calm!

CONNIE. That's not Faces. There's no undercurrent // in Faces.

LINDA. That's how we're doing it now.

CONNIE. OK FINE – I'm giving you one // then.

LINDA. No, you didn't do mine //

CONNIE. No – I'm giving YOU one first, and then I'll do // yours

LINDA. Ok, go.

CONNIE. Ok *(she thinks for a bit)* ok. Anguish…

LINDA. Ok

CONNIE. *(thinking on it)* with an *undercurrent…*of Sexiness.

LINDA. Sexiness?

CONNIE. Uh huh.

LINDA. That's not even a word.

CONNIE. Just do it.

(pause)

LINDA. I don't want to do it, I don't even know what that is.

CONNIE. Just do it and then I'll do yours!

LINDA. Alright, fine. Ok:

*(**LINDA** slowly goes into the anguish.)*

*(It's real anguish. She brings in the erotic longing. It's very painful. They both look at her, it's uncomfortable for everyone. **LINDA** stops playing.)*

There. Ok?

*(She immediately bursts into tears. She covers her eyes. **CONNIE** goes over to her, wraps **LINDA** in her arms. **BRAD** looks at them. **CONNIE** looks over to **BRAD**.)*

CONNIE. *(moved)* This is why I love "faces"

*(**LINDA** gets a hold of herself. She grabs her keys.)*

Where are you going?

LINDA. Get some air.

BRAD. Do you need anything?

*(**LINDA** exits.)*

CONNIE. *(calls after her)* I'll come with you –

*(**TERRY** struts in as she rushes out.)*

TERRY. Valet *service,* just the way I like it, heh heh.

CONNIE. *(rolls her eyes)* Hey Terry.

TERRY. How's the nose Braddyboy? Feelin any better my man?

BRAD. I'm ok.

TERRY. Wha? you mad at me?

BRAD. Nah man, I'm good //

CONNIE. Terry, you look tan //

TERRY. Karen's friend is still lookin for a date tonight, how's about it?

(Long pause)

BRAD. I can't…

TERRY. My treat – I pawned a bum Pontiac off on some old dude last week, I got some extra bread //

BRAD. Thanks man, but I got homework.

TERRY. Why you bein such a dial tone, man?

*(**BRAD** exits to his room.)*

CONNIE. *(excited)* Hey you wanna play Faces? //

(She makes a manic face.)

TERRY. I'm worried about Brad //

CONNIE. I think he thinks I'm attracted to him but I'm not, it's Linda //

TERRY. He's turning into a homebody //

CONNIE. She wants to make it with him.

TERRY. We used to double date all the time, now all he wants to do is cook shit, it's bumming me out.

(He checks his hair in the mirror.)

CONNIE. He was in Vietnam, right?

TERRY. Yeah?

CONNIE. Maybe he's traumatized.

TERRY. Naaah.

CONNIE. A lot of soldiers are traumatized Terry, it's coming out all over the news //

TERRY. Hooa hooa.

*(**TERRY** struts around and does a little dance.)*

CONNIE. How come you weren't drafted?

TERRY. Cuz I'm a lover, not a fighter //

CONNIE. All guys say that and then they beat you black and blue //

TERRY. Daddy just wants a little sugaaaaah! //

CONNIE. My cousin had flat feet but they made him go anyway. *(sad)* Then he blew up.

TERRY. Yeah, well my cousin's copter crashed up in Saigon: BAM, flat as a pancake //

CONNIE. I feel like having pancakes I wonder if there's any batter left? //

TERRY. You want batter? I got batter for you right here, baby //

*(**TERRY** gets behind her, pulls her to him. She pushes him away.)*

CONNIE. Stop it, you're always making moves on me! //

TERRY. Chicks are always mad atcha!

CONNIE. Terry, just go!

(beat)

TERRY. Hey I forgot – I just got back from seein Joey.

CONNIE. *(excited)* Djou get it?

TERRY. Got som'm even better!

(Pats a pocket in his jacket, giggles.)

CONNIE. What do you mean?

TERRY. I'll show ya – wanna sample the goods?

CONNIE. We can't just do it in the middle of my apartment.

TERRY. Let's go in your room.

*(**CONNIE** thinks on it for a moment, nervously.)*

CONNIE. Ok but we gotta hurry, Linda'll freak if she finds out.

*(**TERRY** and **CONNIE** giggle and rush off to their room, shut the door behind them. A beat. Then **LINDA** enters:)*

*(She searches the room for her wallet – finds it eventually between the sofa cushions – puts it in her purse and it about to leave when she overhears laughter coming from **CONNIE**'s room:)*

I've never done it before.

TERRY. Are you kidding me?

CONNIE. No. It's my first time.

(We hear stifled laughter. **LINDA** *covers her mouth. She tiptoes near the door of* **CONNIE***'s room to eavesdrop.)*

TERRY. Well, it's pretty simple. You just stick it up your nose!

*(***LINDA** *looks surprised and a little confused.)*

CONNIE. And then what?

TERRY. Then you snort it down your throat!

*(***LINDA** *looks thoroughly disgusted.)*

CONNIE. I'm scared.

TERRY. Gimme your nose, I'll stick it in for you!

CONNIE. *(frightened)* My nose-holes are too small!

TERRY. Well I'm here to feel good. I thought that's what you wanted too.

CONNIE. *(sad)* How can I feel good when I have all this white stuff coming out my nostrils!?

LINDA. *(feeling sick) Oh my god.*

TERRY. *(angry)* Gimme your head!

CONNIE. *(terrified)* Forget it, I changed my mind –

*(***LINDA** *looks terrified, she doesn't know whether to barge in or not.)*

*(***LINDA** *squeezes her eyes shut. We hear quiet tussling offstage, then eventual silence.)*

TERRY. Now how do you feel?

CONNIE. *(sad)* It's burning.

*(***LINDA** *opens her eyes; she looks as if she could cry.)*

TERRY. I told you you'd love it.

CONNIE. *(devastated)* It's dripping down my throat.

TERRY. I gotta run. I got a hot date tonight.

(**TERRY** *opens the door, catching* **LINDA** *off guard. She poses extemporaneously against the wall and arranges the leaves of a plant.)*

Hey Linda, gotta book.

(**TERRY** *exits, slams the door behind him.* **LINDA** *hesitantly goes to* **CONNIE***'s door.)*

LINDA. *(softly)* Connie? *(knocks quietly on the door)* Connie are you ok?

CONNIE. *(os) I'm not getting you a ticket to the concert!*

LINDA. I don't care about that anymore honey… I just want to make sure you're alright.

CONNIE. *(os, a little manic from the coke)* I'M FINE. *(she sniffles)*

LINDA. You don't sound fine.

(**CONNIE** *sniffles.)*

CONNIE. *(os)* I'm blowing my hair now.

(We hear the blow dryer. **BRAD** *enters, searching for something.)*

BRAD. Hey Linda, back already?

LINDA. *(clearly upset)* I forgot something.

BRAD. Have you seen my pastry bag anywhere? I'm practicing pate choux.

LINDA. No.

(**BRAD** *notices the state she's in.)*

BRAD. What's wrong?

(A pause, as **LINDA** *tries to hold it together.)*

Linda –

(Then – she impulsively turns to **BRAD***:)*

LINDA. *(in tears, blurts)* You can't just shove your thing into any hole you *want*! Some holes aren't meant for that and I think it's – *disgusting*.

(**BRAD** *is a deer in the headlights.)*

BRAD. *(panicking)* Ok well I'm gonna look for my pastry bag –

(**BRAD** *starts to leave.* **LINDA**, *clocking his anxiety:)*

LINDA. WAIT A MINUTE –

(**BRAD** *freezes,* **LINDA** *accosts him.)*

Are you hiding something?

BRAD. *(lame denial)* No –

LINDA. Yes you are. Brad, I can see right through you.

(**BRAD** *reacts)*

LINDA. You think I don't know what's going on in my own house? It's perverted!

BRAD. N-nothing's going on *here* – I would never do that here.

LINDA. *(confused)* You!?

(**BRAD** *is stymied.)*

BRAD. Yeah?

LINDA. *So then it's not just Terry?*

(**BRAD** *reacts.)*

BRAD. *(short circuiting)* Terry –?!

LINDA. *(icily)* So this is what you two do on your "double dates"?

BRAD. *No I've never done that with him, I swear.*

LINDA. But you've done it. You've done this to someone's *face*!

(**BRAD** *is discombobulated.)*

BRAD. I can't talk about this with you.

LINDA. *(nearly in tears)* I'm sick…you're making me sick to my stomach.

(Long pause)

BRAD. *(shame)* Don't look at me like that.

(pause)

(crumbling) Don't look at me like that!

(pause)

(deeply pained) I tried to fix myself *but I can't. (a quiet admission:)* Sometimes I don't even want to live anymore.

(pause)

LINDA. *(quiet, heartbroken) What kind of world is this?* Why do people do these…terrible things? I can't… I can't… It's so…*horrible…*

(Long pause as she tries to recover.)

(grave concern) Brad… I had a friend who sipped soda up her nose through a straw. She had to go to the hospital!

*(**BRAD** reacts.)*

BRAD. *(trying to normalize)* Linda, I know this must be… disorienting for you. But it does feel good being honest. Maybe this could be a new beginning –

LINDA. *(horrified) How can you say that!?*

BRAD. No, you're right! You're right. I can fix it – I will! *(beat)* I'll fix it, ok?

LINDA. *(wipes her tears)* I guess I'm naïve. I didn't know men did these things.

(pause)

BRAD. It happens a lot on the beach.

LINDA. *(envisioning it)* The *beach?*

BRAD. At night. Also in alleyways.

*(**LINDA** has the whole scenario in her head. She's completely flummoxed.)*

LINDA. But…does it even *fit?*

BRAD. *(shy)* You make it fit, I don't know… Things just… expand. *(pause)* I feel weird talking about this with you.

LINDA. *(trying to normalize)* That's ok. *(beat)* I left something at work, I should go now, before they close.

BRAD. You're not mad at me?

LINDA. *(gingerly, but not entirely sympathetic)* No – *no* Brad. You – go look for your pastry bag…

*(***BRAD*** wipes tears from his eyes. She exits, unsmiling.* ***BRAD*** *watches her leave. He looks worried. He's still like this for a bit. He sighs, drained, covers his face. He sits down on the sofa, incredibly forlorn.)*

*(***CONNIE*** whisks into the room like a sirocco all coked up and wearing a brand new foxy outfit; she's rooting around for something. Her hair is blown out and looks very Farrah.* ***BRAD*** *wipes tears quickly, tries to cover.)*

CONNIE. Hey Brad. *(She sniffles.)*

BRAD. Hey Connie, excited for your date?

CONNIE. *(She moves her jaw around.)* Have you seen my earring lying around? I keep losing my clip-ons. I wonder if I should get my ears pierced, that way I could keep track of things. Everything is so elusive to me.

BRAD. What's wrong with your jaw?

CONNIE. You're just like my brother You're always asking questions.

BRAD. You have a brother?

CONNIE. I love being asked things, it makes me feel so alive. Ask me another!

BRAD. What time's your date?

CONNIE. You remind me so much of my brother. He's a stickler for facts, but he loses the big picture But that's his loss. *(Beat, she notices he's down.)* Brad, is everything ok? //

BRAD. I'm just tired //

CONNIE. My brother was tired too; I should get ready. George is a stickler for punctual girls; I mean I only met him fifteen minutes ago, but you know what they say.

BRAD. *(real concern)* Connie, you sure this concert's a good idea?

CONNIE. What do you mean?

BRAD. You don't even know this guy.

CONNIE. *(a little defensive)* George is sweet. He likes me.

BRAD. *(tentative)* I'm sure he likes // you but

CONNIE. *(weakly)* I think he's a stand up guy.

BRAD. *(unconvinced)* Maybe you're right. It's none of my business.

(She looks over at **BRAD** *– a little sad and crumpled up on the sofa. She musters courage, then:)*

CONNIE. *(gingerly)* Brad? Why do you always keep falling? Is there some insupportable weight you're carrying? I mean…*inside*?

BRAD. *(lame denial)* I don't know what you mean.

(She shifts a little closer to him.)

CONNIE. *(gentle confrontation)* Brad… I know what's going on.

BRAD. *(defeated)* Linda told you?

CONNIE. Linda doesn't have to *tell* me, I can see it on your face.

BRAD. *(suddenly self conscious)* Really?

CONNIE. Brad, you're traumatized! It's all over the news!

*(***BRAD** *reacts.)*

You can stop trying to hide your secret from me. I just want to help. *(she approaches him delicately)* No one is born like this, Brad.

BRAD. *(reacts)* Then why am I *like* this?

CONNIE. *(flummoxed by his ignorance)* Because Oriental people have been shooting at you!

BRAD. *(confused)* I don't think that's it...

CONNIE. *(sighs sadly)* You're in denial I saw that on the news too.

BRAD. *(a spasm of rage and frustration)* CONNIE, I JUST WANT TO BE WITH A *WOMAN*!

CONNIE. *(sweetly stroking his arm)* Shhh… Just keep reliving the trauma.

BRAD. *(confused)* What trauma? //

CONNIE. *(soothing)* Shhh... Brad, you're gonna find someone great. *(an epiphany)* And then Linda could babysit. I mean she's bad with kids *but people can change.*

(pause)

BRAD. *(tentative, sad)* Do you think *I* can change?

CONNIE. You just have to keep trying. Don't give into these feelings.

(She clicks her jaw. **BRAD** *is nonplussed. He starts to leave.)*

BRAD. I'm gonna finish unpacking –

*(***CONNIE** *grabs him, pulls him down next to her.)*

CONNIE. Look, I understand what you're going through, Brad //

BRAD. You *don't* //

CONNIE. Yes I *do...*

BRAD. When I got back from the war I went to my family and told them about me. *(long pause)* And they... *(broken)* They told me to go...*kill* myself.

(pause)

CONNIE. *(moved)* How can they say that? *(contemplative)* Maybe they're communist sympathizers.

BRAD. *(stymied by her response)* I gotta go.

*(***BRAD** *is about to get up,* **CONNIE** *stops him.)*

CONNIE. I've never told anyone this before but... *(blurts)* I have these same feelings that you have.

*(***BRAD** *short circuits with complete puzzlement.)*

BRAD. *(confused)* But you date *guys* – a *lot* of guys!

(pause)

CONNIE. *(very vulnerable)* Look. I had something...happen to me once...with a guy. He wasn't good to me. *(long pause)* And since then I keep telling myself if I find some guy to love me it'll be fine... But it doesn't work.

(pause)

BRAD. Does Linda know?

(She shakes her head.)

(badly concealing his disbelief) Have you met any…*girls* that you *like*?

CONNIE. *(confused)* Yeah. On the beach.

BRAD. So…you've *been* with them?

CONNIE. *(matter of fact)* Just today I was with someone. It felt nice. I love getting all wet.

*(**BRAD** reacts.)*

BRAD. Have you ever been in love?

CONNIE. No. No one's ever told me they loved me except for my father. And he's a minister they'll say anything.

*(Pause; she sees forlorn looking **BRAD**.)*

You can *change,* Brad.

*(**BRAD** looks at her, struggling to find some optimism.)*

BRAD. Sometimes…it's so stupid but I feel like something's possible. *(raw, open)* I want something…*beautiful*…for my *life*…

*(**CONNIE**, moved, grabs his hand, squeezes it. He looks at her, it's heartbreaking. They have a moment of true – or they think it's true – connection. Possesed by boldness, **BRAD** kisses **CONNIE** – awkwardly – his heart isn't in it. He gets on top of her, removes the top of her dress, unbuttons his shirt.)*

CONNIE. Brad – wait, this…this just feels…

BRAD. I know…

(He climbs off her, dispirited by failure.)

(quiet and awkward) Sorry…

CONNIE. It's ok. *(pause, then sweetly)* I just think if you can imagine Oriental people shooting you you'll see better results.

*(**BRAD** nods, trying to hide his puzzlement. They hug. The front door flings open.* ***LINDA*** *enters with a bouquet of orchids.)*

LINDA. I got zebra // orchids –

BRAD. Linda –

(She takes in the scene. Then drops the orchids, rushes off to her room. She slams the door. **CONNIE** *sighs.* **BRAD** *shuts his eyes for a moment, bereft, exhausted. Eventually he resumes buttoning his shirt.* **CONNIE** *picks up the orchids, replaces the dead ones in the vase with these. Goes to the door.)*

CONNIE. Linda – nothing happened! Linda? //

*(**LINDA** opens the door and shoves a bra at* **CONNIE**.*)*

LINDA. You left your bra on my bed.

CONNIE. That's not my bra.

LINDA. Then why was it on my bed?

CONNIE. Because I don't put other people's bras on my bed. *I put them on other people's beds!*

(pause)

LINDA. *(betrayed)* So do I have to start wearing a nose guard in my own house?

CONNIE. *(confused)* Only if you want.

LINDA. Now I feel like you're all staring at my nostrils! I can't live like this!

BRAD. *(confused)* We're not...doing – that.

LINDA. *(sarcasm)* Oh no, not *you.*

*(**BRAD** and* **CONNIE** *exchange a confused look.* **LINDA** *puts on a disco record – "Too Hot to Handle" by Giorgio Moroder. She grabs a doorknob of a door and "dances" with the door as a substitute for a partner. As this is happening,* **BRAD** *exits to his room.)*

BRAD. Well. I'm gonna finish unpacking.

LINDA. Good!

CONNIE. No – Brad, she's just –

(He exits into his room, slams the door.)

Don't say "good" – that's really rude.

LINDA. *(dancing)* I'm not talking to you.

(She dances. **CONNIE** *watches, penitent.)*

CONNIE. *(pleadingly)* Nothing happened, ok? *(***LINDA** *ignores her)* Brad is sweet. He understands me. *(***LINDA** *ignores her)* No one understands me...but he *does.* *(***LINDA** *ignores her)* He knows me now. *(***LINDA** *ignores her)* You and I don't really know each other... Maybe we can be close. *(***LINDA** *continues to ignore her;* **CONNIE** *feels completely stranded)* It's scary to get close to people but it can be healing...

*(***LINDA** *continues to dance.)*

Linda? ...Please talk to me...

*(***LINDA** *continues to dance.* **CONNIE** *is in tears.)*

Linda //

LINDA. *(mean) WHY DON'T YOU GO AIR OUT YOUR NOSE HOLES*!

*(***LINDA** *dances more fervently.* **CONNIE** *doesn't know how to respond to this, or even if it's an insult. She exits into kitchen.* **LINDA** *dances, upset.)*

(She dances like this for a while. **CONNIE** *enters the living room.)*

CONNIE. Brad?

*(***BRAD** *enters.)*

Is this your pastry bag?

(She produces pastry bag)

BRAD. Great – can I have that?

(He goes to get it but she pulls it away.)

CONNIE. Only if you dance with me first.

*(**LINDA** rolls her eyes, dances.)*

BRAD. *(worn out)* I don't really feel like dancing.

*(**CONNIE** starts disco dancing insouciantly.)*

Connie, I have homework.

*(**CONNIE** dances at him. She dangles the pastry bag at him as a lure. She starts doing The Bump with **LINDA**.)*

LINDA. *Excuse me //*

CONNIE. That's ok.

*(She keeps forcing The Bump on **LINDA**.)*

LINDA. Can you go dance over there? //

CONNIE. No The floor is crooked Anyway I like it near the plant!

*(She dances excitedly near the plant. **LINDA** rolls her eyes, ignores her.)*

BRAD. Fine I'll dance for a minute ok?

*(**CONNIE** dances energetically over to him. They freestyle.)*

*(This goes on for a while. **BRAD** starts to really enjoy himself. **CONNIE** alternates doing The Bump with **LINDA** and **BRAD**. She bumps **LINDA** one time too many.)*

LINDA. DIDN'T I SAY I'M NOT TALKING TO YOU!?

*(She violently swipes the needle off the record, rushes into **BRAD**'s room, slams the door.)*

CONNIE. *(beaming)* We're like a real *family* now.

*(**MRS. WICKER** enters the apartment, frantic, holding an envelope and a quill.)*

MRS. WICKER. Oh god. I tried to do the calligraphy myself. *Where's Linda?*

CONNIE. What's the matter?

MRS. WICKER. It looks horrible, *I'm not a fucking calligrapher!*

BRAD. *(calls out)* Linda!

*(**LINDA** enters.)*

MRS. WICKER. *(to **LINDA**)* I'm ruining the whole invitation.

CONNIE. It doesn't look so bad.

LINDA. Do you have your medication?

MRS. WICKER. *(whispering)* Don't say it in front of *them – I don't want them to know...*

BRAD. *(to **LINDA**)* What kind of medication?

LINDA. She won't take it //

MRS. WICKER. I might have a nervous breakdown!

CONNIE. *(intimidated)* (Do you wanna see my new coat?)

MRS. WICKER. *(re: the stucco, panic) There's a lot of dimensions coming out at me!!!*

BRAD. *(leads her to the sofa)* Mrs. Wicker, why don't you sit down.

MRS. WICKER. Who's he?

CONNIE. That's Brad, you met him this morning //

MRS. WICKER. *(rankled)* He's wearing pants! //

BRAD. *(very sweetly)* Everything's gonna be alright //

MRS. WICKER. *You're just a gay, what do you know*!!!

*(**BRAD** is stung. **MR. WICKER** enters. **LINDA** is noticeably discomfited. She goes to the bar. She unscrews the cap off a bottle.)*

WICKER. What's all this racket //

CONNIE. We're making her take pills //

MRS. WICKER. I'm doing the calligraphy myself.

WICKER. For what? //

MRS. WICKER. BETTY'S SHOWER //

LINDA. *(to **BRAD**)* Open her purse //

*(**BRAD** doesn't respond.)*

MRS. WICKER. I can't breathe.

LINDA. Brad!

*(**BRAD** is out of it. **LINDA**, annoyed, gets the bottle herself – **CONNIE** grabs it from her. **LINDA** reacts.)*

CONNIE. I'll take one okay And if I can take one can you take one too?

MRS. WICKER. *(vulnerable)* Like the matching grants…? Like you hear about on public radio…?

LINDA. *(feeling left out)* I listen to public radio.

CONNIE. You won't be afraid will you?

MRS. WICKER. *(frightened)* I could go into narcosis //

CONNIE. *(plainly)* Fine lets go into narcosis together.

*(On the word "together" **CONNIE** takes a pill.)*

LINDA. Connie are you sure that's safe? //

CONNIE. I get anxiety attacks also.

*(She swallows it down with water, then hands **MRS. WICKER** a pill. **MRS. WICKER** looks at it for a moment, then nervously swallows the pill.)*

See, you're not having a nervous breakdown // are you?

MRS. WICKER. *(hysterically impatient) I don't know what I'm having.*

WICKER. *(dismissive)* She's fine.

MRS. WICKER. You just want to buy my plot before the rates go up.

LINDA. *(desperate)* Do you want me to help you with invitations, I could do stamps //

MRS. WICKER. *(to **LINDA**, suddenly transformed)* You know I feel a heck of a lot better!

LINDA. Do you feel it working?

MRS. WICKER. You can't even hear me can // you.

LINDA. I can //

MRS. WICKER. It must be awful to be deaf in one ear you must feel so imbalanced If I were deaf I would rather it be in both ears Being half deaf does not appeal to me // Being

LINDA. I //

MRS. WICKER. half anything I want to be *whole*! I know that seems impractical to you but you're a pragmatist I'm a dreamer my forebears *built this country* //

CONNIE. I was in *Miracle Worker* in high school //

MRS. WICKER. That's nice Connie //

LINDA. Do you feel well enough to go upstairs? //

MRS. WICKER. No and I want to finish the calligraphy on this one invitation. *(She picks up the invitation, rage)* OH I SCREWED THE WHOLE THING UP. *(She picks up the quill, then benignly)* (I only have the zip code There.)

(She finishes the invitation.)

BRAD. I could lick envelopes.

MR. WICKER. *(makes a "swishy" gesture)* Lick envelopes, mmmm.

MRS. WICKER. I was thinking of making that casserole you like Henry //

MR. WICKER. I don't like casserole

MRS. WICKER. Not even your favorite // one?

MR. WICKER. I don't *have* a favorite one! //

MRS. WICKER. *(her truest moment)* You think I want to be cooking for you? You think I don't regret every minute of this marriage?

(This cuts to the bone, they all feel it. A pause and then –)

MR. WICKER. *(sheepish)* I like...the one with the broccoli.

MRS. WICKER. *(elated)* That's *my* favorite too the one with the *broccoli.* I'll make that one then, I knew you had a favorite.

(She hugs him.)

You're a keeper!

(She exits.)

(tense silence)

*(**CONNIE** crosses to the door.)*

CONNIE. I'm going to help her with stamps

LINDA. *(dirty look)* I'M HELPING WITH STAMPS!

*(**LINDA** exits, slams the door. **WICKER** looks at **CONNIE**.)*

CONNIE. Er. I'm going to read – Linda's book.

(She looks for a book lying around, can't find one, exits into the kitchen.)

*(**BRAD** and **MR. WICKER** are left. **BRAD** looks over at **MR. WICKER**.)*

MR. WICKER. You givin me the thermometer?

*(**BRAD** reacts.)*

You do and I'll knock you flat on your ASS!
HA HA HA HA
Nah I'm kiddin, I'm kiddin ya.

BRAD. You're…not my type Mr. Wicker.

MR. WICKER. Whaddaya mean not your type, whose type am I?

(beat)

I was middleweight champ in the 64th

BRAD. 64th what?

MR. WICKER. Battalion!

BRAD. You were in a war?

MR. WICKER. I was in *the* war, once I was in Auschwitz, no not Auschwitz – oh *Dresden* – oh man that was a stinkhole, and we bombed those krauts to hell the fuckers. That was a great time to be alive. Full of streamers and tickertape parades and atom bombs and mushroom clouds rippling out on the horizon. Were you in the army Brad?

BRAD. Yeah // I

MR. WICKER. Or navy? – you'd be cookin with gas there heh heh. "Anchors aweigh!"

(He flutters his eyelashes prissily.)

BRAD. I was drafted actually.

MR. WICKER. *(faggy singing, floppy wrists)* "In the na-vy!"

BRAD. *(quietly)* Something like that.

MR. WICKER. Nah, I'm kiddin – any fag that wants to kill a bunch a japs is ok by me. Nam, now that was a great war, so they burned a few gooks. Those hippies make me sick. First they go and crucify Nixon, then they go and stick some douchebag pean*ut* farmer in the oval office. It's a sad day for America.

(beat)

Hey did you hear what the faggot said to the other faggot in the bar as he passed by?

*(**BRAD** smiles politely.)*

BRAD. No, I didn't //

MR. WICKER. "Can I push your stool in for you?" *(He laughs at his own joke.)*

BRAD. *(forced smile)* That's a good // one.

MR. WICKER. I got another one: What's the difference between a microwave and a gay guy? A microwave won't brown your *meat*! Heh heh heh heh.

*(**BRAD** smiles politely.)*

(smiles) you don't mind me takin the piss out of you Brad.

BRAD. Actually I // should

MR. WICKER. Cause if you do I'll *beat ya fuckin head in ya faggot!! (beat)* HA HA HA I'm *kidding*, I'm slappin your toe. You'd like that wouldn't you, me slappin your toe, heh heh, I know what you dirty fags are all thinkin.

(pause)

BRAD. When in Greece, uh – how do you…how do you separate the men from the boys?

MR. WICKER. How?

(pause)

BRAD. With a crowbar.

(**MR. WICKER** *laughs.)*

MR. WICKER. That's a good one.

(beat)

BRAD. What do faggots call hemorrhoids?

MR. WICKER. A night out? HA HA HA HA

BRAD. Speed bumps.

(**WICKER** *laughs jovially. He's relaxed, he's pretty open.)*

MR. WICKER. You know, you and me should mosey on down to the Rolley Pony on Tuesday – it's Bingo Night. Whaddayou say?

(pause)

Whaddayou say Brad, you and me?

(**BRAD** *appears to be increasingly sick, lost. There's a pause, then he forces a tiny smile. He looks up at* **WICKER**. *He nods, complaisant.)*

BRAD. Okay.

(**WICKER** *smiles.)*

MR. WICKER. I'll buy you a Lancer's. Last week I won three bucks. *(beat; he stands)* Well time for a feeding, Mrs. Wicker's got some slop in the trough –

(**WICKER** *opens the door to exit,* **MRS. WICKER** *is standing in the doorway.)*

MRS. WICKER. *(kind of drugged)* I just wanted to say I really like my pill. I feel like new vistas are opening up for me.

MR. WICKER. Cmon Phyllis, the food'll get cold.

MRS. WICKER. Cold: Just like my marriage. *(She looks around at them. No one laughs. This upsets her greatly.)* You know what'll be funny? When we evict you because you didn't pay your *fucking rent.*

(She laughs at this. **LINDA** *enters.)*

LINDA. I'm done with the stamps.

MRS. WICKER. Thanks for the saliva. Lin.

*(**MR. & MRS. WICKER** exeunt. **LINDA** looks over at **BRAD**. **BRAD** has the same frozen, sickened expression on his face. **LINDA** tries to dismiss this; she goes to the bar and pours herself a giant drink.)*

LINDA. I took a walk before. On the beach? *(pause)* There was a band playing. The sun was starting to set The water was all pink. *(pause)* The music was so beautiful. *(pause)* And... I don't know. *(pause, a little forced)* Mrs. Wicker finished up all the invitations, isn't that great? It's good to feel useful. *(pause)* I've never been up there before, the apartment is really nice. *(pause, she turns to **BRAD**, brimming with ineffable sadness)* I'm starting to understand life now... *I know what this world is. (pause)* All this time I thought... *(she trails off; then, with strained optimism)* It's not what I wanted, but that doesn't matter. *(pause; a sickly smile)* Nobody wants to be alone. *(**BRAD** doesn't respond. Her smile drops. She goes over to him, solemn)* Look, whatever you do is your business. Just don't hurt anyone.

(pause)

BRAD. *(oddly vacant)* You have nothing to worry about.

*(**LINDA**'s expression changes.)*

LINDA. *(hopeful) Really?*

*(**BRAD** stares right through her. It's a little eerie.)*

BRAD. *(cold)* Pour me one.

*(**LINDA** demurs, then pours him a scotch. **BRAD** downs it.)*

*(**CONNIE** enters. She rearranges the orchids.)*

LINDA. These apartments are all pretty nice compared to what's out there //

CONNIE. *(sings to herself)*

("LIMBO, LIMBO") //

LINDA. Maybe we can redecorate. I like it here.

*(**CONNIE**'s expression changes. She stares at the orchids, somewhat trancelike.)*

CONNIE. Linda…didn't you just get these?

LINDA. Yeah.

CONNIE. *(quietly unnerved)* But they're…already dying.

*(**LINDA** walks over to **CONNIE**. She looks at the flowers. Her expression changes. Long pause.)*

LINDA. *(increasingly disconcerted, lost)* Well. I'll…get new ones… From the shop.

*(**LINDA** gets very still, she looks like she could be sick. **BRAD** and **CONNIE** look at her.)*

CONNIE. *(quietly)* Linda…?

*(**LINDA** starts to shake.)*

(Tears well up in her eyes; she's a terrified little girl.)

*(**BRAD** and **CONNIE** shift their attention to her.)*

(An inexplicable, inescapable horror sets in. They all feel it.)

(It's eerily quiet.)

BRAD. Is everything ok?

*(**LINDA** has gotten very faraway, then notices they're staring at her.)*

LINDA. *(forces a tiny smile)* Look at you two, aw, don't worry about me.

(No one's convinced.)

(sickly smile) I just – feel a little funny, I don't know.

*(She sits down on the sofa next to **BRAD**.)*

CONNIE. *(wishing away the terror)* Maybe you – need a vacation. Brad, have you ever heard of this place, Love Canal?

LINDA. Connie, it's a toxic waste site!

(beat)

CONNIE. *(weakly, but still trying)* Maybe there's discounts.

LINDA. I don't care about discounts.

(beat)

CONNIE. *(shaken)* America has…so many freedoms Linda. You…really should try them out…

LINDA. *(struggling to normalize)* Maybe I need to eat something.

BRAD. *(unnerved)* Why don't I make us Pasta a la Brad.

LINDA. *(a little manic)* Connie he's gonna cook for us, did you hear that?

CONNIE. I'm not the one who's half-deaf, Linda.

BRAD. Ok, let's see – do you have onions? //

CONNIE. No.

BRAD. Garlic? //

CONNIE. All we have is Fritos.

LINDA. We can order in //

*(**LINDA** forages for take out menus in an end-table drawer. The tenor starts to shift, gets more manic.)*

CONNIE. I want Chinese!

LINDA. Chinese food is so fattening.

CONNIE. No it's not!

LINDA. it's dripping in oil!

CONNIE. *You don't need to lose weight!*

LINDA. Will you stop shaking your boobs at me!?

BRAD. *(to **CONNIE**)* Wait, I thought you were going to the concert //

CONNIE. *(sudden realization)* Where's George, he was supposed to be here at seven!

*(**LINDA** shakes her boobs at **CONNIE**.)*

Stop putting your things on me Linda //

LINDA. YOU'RE PUTTING // YOUR THINGS ON *ME*

CONNIE. *I'M SICK AND TIRED OF IT!*

BRAD. Girls come on.

(He gets them together in a huddle.)

Let's not fight. *(they look at each other, deliberating this)* Let's really be a *family* //

CONNIE. But distant.

BRAD. Ok //

CONNIE. And I want her to teach me new dances //

LINDA. Ok, but you have to spend more time // with me!

CONNIE. Let's go shopping tomorrow, we can go to Melrose //

BRAD. I wanna go to Melrose// too.

CONNIE. LET'S PLAY FACES!

BRAD. Oh you wanna play Faces huh? What about this face? *(makes a face)* What about *this* face?

*(**BRAD** makes a whole bunch of faces. **CONNIE** cracks up. As he makes faces, **LINDA** finds a fugitive envelope hidden in the cushion of the sofa, opens it.)*

CONNIE. *(bounces on the sofa, delighted)* HOOA HOOA!

BRAD. *(to **CONNIE**, maniacally playful)* WHAT ABOUT THIS FACE?

(He's a giraffe, a penguin, a puppy.)

CONNIE. That's good but it's not technically Faces. *(to herself)* But maybe corruption is the soul of invention // *(shrugs)*

LINDA. Connie, I thought you paid this!

*(**LINDA** righteously holds up the envelope.)*

CONNIE. *(sheepish)* I bought a hair clip.

LINDA. You were supposed to send this two weeks ago, now they're gonna shut off the phone service.

CONNIE. *(quietly)* Sorry Linda.

LINDA. *(trying to remain civil)* Connie, you really need to look for something.

CONNIE. *(taking this literally) What?*

LINDA. A JOB.

BRAD. *(to **LINDA**)* Look, Terry owes me some dough, I can just hit him up //

LINDA. We can't go shopping tomorrow, we need to pool our money! How are we gonna make rent? *(**CONNIE** mimics her last line she says it)* You heard what Wicker said we – *(**BRAD** has become an orangutang)* – Brad be serious.

*(He chases **LINDA** around the room in an orangutan fashion and tickles her.)*

BRAD. *(making orangutan noises)* OO OO OO OO AAA AAA

*(**LINDA** laughs hysterically as **BRAD** tickles her.)*

LINDA. Stop – stop it Brad – AHHHHH

*(As **BRAD** and **LINDA** tussle, **CONNIE** hops over the stereo and resumes playing "Too Hot to Handle" – she bops along to the music mindlessly. This goes on for a little bit.)*

*(**LINDA** runs into the kitchen to escape, and **BRAD** runs after her – as he does the swinging door from the kitchen bashes him in the face.)*

CONNIE. Brad!

*(She pulls the needle off the record. **LINDA** rushes back in. **BRAD**'s holding his head. He grabs some tissues.)*

BRAD. Somebody has to fix this.

LINDA. *(sympathetic)* There's nothing wrong with the door, you // just

BRAD. *(an attack)* Well there's nothing wrong with *me*!

(beat)

LINDA. Nobody's // saying

BRAD. Do you *want* me to get hurt? *Somebody has to FIX THIS!*

(beat)

CONNIE. It doesn't look that bad… It's just a little –

*(In one quick sweep **BRAD** impulsively swipes a bunch of trouvailles off a nearby endtable. A*

long, painfully uncomfortable silence. **BRAD** *grows increasingly ashamed, penitent.* **BRAD** *quietly bends down and cleans the small mess he made.)*

BRAD. *(quiet, tiny)* I apologize.

LINDA. *(moved)* Do you need ice?

(pause)

BRAD. I'm ok.

(They sit like this for a long uncomfortable while. **CONNIE** *is increasingly deperate to puncture the awful silence.)*

CONNIE. You guys wanna see my coat?

*(***CONNIE** *sheepishly, tentatively, exits to her room, then re-enters wearing her coat. It is the most nondescript coat imaginable.)*

Look, look at the cut and the whole inside is synthetic, I mean not synthetic but it's this new fabric, it's a combination of I think like plastic and wool – it's water resistant, it's totally cute. Not plastic and wool, I don't know what it is. But.

(pause)

And its water resistant, I could wear it out, I could wear it at night, it's good for when there's breezes.

(She looks at herself in the mirror – her smile starts to evaporate.)

The fabric is, it traps breezes somehow, I don't know the salesgirl explained it to me, she told me I looked really great in it.

(beat)

It's a big deal that I got this coat. I usually don't buy myself things, I like to buy things for other people.

(beat)

I could wear it out, I could wear it around.

CONNIE. I love the zippers. They zip up they zip down, it's so versatile OH – and you can wear this coat with anything.

(STOP)

it zips up it zips down.

(STOP)

it

zips up

it zips

(pause)

down

(Tears well up in her eyes.)

(quiet, shame) I hate it…

I hate my coat…

(Doorbell rings.)

(Doorbell rings again.)

*(***LINDA*** finally answers. She's visibly shaken.)*

(It's **TERRY***.)*

TERRY. Where'd you get that doormat I need a doormat.

CONNIE. *(to herself)* Men like doormats.

TERRY. What?

LINDA. Sears //

TERRY. That's rad, I have a sears credit, I'll check it out What's shakin Braddy-boy?

(He twirls the tacky gold chain around his neck)

BRAD. *(affectless)* Hi Terry.

TERRY. *(to* **CONNIE***)* What's the matter with you?

CONNIE. *(teary-eyed)* I don't like my coat.

TERRY. So return it.

CONNIE. *It was a sale item.*

(pause)

TERRY. *(spots something)* I think there's gum in this.

(No one responds.)

Hello?

(No one responds.)

(naughty smile) So "how's the living situation"? Are you guys "having fun"? Heheheh

(They all seem on the edge of suicide.)

(He ribs **BRAD**. **BRAD** *smiles a sickly smile.)*

Heh heh.

(pause)

This place is like a funeral home, lighten up bitches! I'm hittin' the Pony, I'm gonna play pool, I gotta date tonight, Tina's a total fox –

BRAD. Tina. What happened to Karen?

TERRY. Who?

BRAD. Karen.

TERRY. Oh she came down with the clap but Tina's foxy, she's Karen's friend. Remember I was telling you about Tina? and she's got a friend Lucy total fox fuckin hourglass hips Whaddaya say Braddy-o?

*(***BRAD** *doesn't answer.)*

The hourglass?

*(***BRAD** *doesn't answer.)*

Sands of time, flip her upside down watch the sands trickle down ha ha ha…whaddaya say.

LINDA. *(reading double meanings into everything)* He's reading a *book*!

CONNIE. Yeah!

TERRY. Reading a book? What the fuck is that supposed to mean, it's Saturday night.

*(**TERRY** looks at him expectantly. **BRAD** doesn't say anything. Then – eventually, a concession.)*

BRAD. Ok.

TERRY. Serious? I'll call Tina.

BRAD. Ok, let me get my stuff.

*(He stands, walks towards his room, when **TERRY** calls out:)*

TERRY. C'mon y'little faggot. *(**TERRY** laughs. He slaps his knee like he's calling a dog)* "coomme on!" "coooome on faggot, getcha stuff heh heh"

*(**TERRY** cracks up – this is the funniest joke he's ever heard. He goes over to him.)*

*(**TERRY** pokes at him playfully, pokes at him, pokes at him, laughing. **BRAD** looks right at him, just takes it. The humiliation builds and builds.)*

"C'mon faggot!"

BRAD. *(plainly)* I am a faggot.

*(**TERRY**'s expression slowly changes.)*

TERRY. What?

*(**BRAD** looks at him. He looks like he could cry. He's shuddering. He can barely breathe.)*

Dude, what the fuck's your problem?

BRAD. *(hoarsely)* I… I… I love you.

(pause)

TERRY. *(confused)* You –?

*(**BRAD** bursts into anguished, racking sobs. He sobs and sobs and they just stare at him, blankly.)*

*(His sobs transmogrify into laughter. The laughter builds, becomes hysterical. It's a little too hysterical. **CONNIE** starts to laugh with him.)*

CONNIE. *(trying to be funny)* I'm a faggot too!

(She laughs hysterically. **TERRY** *and* **LINDA** *crack smiles. The smiles turn into laughter.)*

TERRY. Yeah, me too.

LINDA. *We're all faggots!*

(The laughter builds, grows more hysterical.)

TERRY. I'M A FAGGOT!

(Laughter grows wild, manic. Tears streaming down their faces.)

CONNIE. *(excitedly) BOB HOPE'S A FAGGOT!*

(Laughter is pitched even higher.)

(This goes on for a while.)

(Eventually, **BRAD** *stops laughing. He pulls himself off the floor. The rest of them are still going.* **BRAD**, *unsmiling, wipes the tears from his eyes. He sits on a chair. Removed, but not too deliberately. The laughter dies down.)*

(As they recover a disquieting, awful dread creeps into the room.)

(silence)

(black)